I0760456

ASUNDER

THE HOUSE OF CRIMSON & CLOVER VOLUME VI

SARAH M. CRADIT

Cover Design by Sarah M. Cradit
Editing by Shaner Media Creations

First Edition
ISBN-10: 1505561558
ISBN-13: 978-1505561555

Publisher Contact:
sarah@sarahmcradit.com
www.sarahmcradit.com

ALSO BY SARAH M. CRADIT

KINGDOM OF THE WHITE SEA

Kingdom of the White Sea Trilogy

The Kingless Crown

The Broken Realm

The Hidden Kingdom

The Book of All Things

The Raven and the Rush

The Sylvan and the Sand

The Altruist and the Assassin

The Melody and the Master

The Claw and the Crowned

THE SAGA OF CRIMSON & CLOVER

The House of Crimson and Clover Series

The Storm and the Darkness

Shattered

The Illusions of Eventide

Bound

Midnight Dynasty

Asunder

Empire of Shadows

Myths of Midwinter

The Hinterland Veil

The Secrets Amongst the Cypress

Within the Garden of Twilight

House of Dusk, House of Dawn

Midnight Dynasty Series

A Tempest of Discovery

A Storm of Revelations

A Torrent of Deceit

The Seven Series

1970

1972

1973

1974

1975

1976

1980

Vampires of the Merovingi Series

The Island

and more

The Dusk Trilogy

St. Charles at Dusk: The Story of Oz and Adrienne

Flourish: The Story of Anne Fontaine

Banshee: The Story of Giselle Deschanel

Crimson & Clover Stories

Surrender: The Story of Oz and Ana

Shame: The Story of Jonathan St. Andrews

Fire & Ice: The Story of Remy & Fleur

Dark Blessing: The Landry Triplets

Pandora's Box: The Story of Jasper & Pandora

The Menagerie: Oriana's Den of Iniquities

A Band of Heather: The Story of Colleen and Noah

The Ephemeral: The Story of Autumn & Gabriel

Bayou's Edge: The Landry Triplets

For more information, and exciting bonus material, visit www.sarahmcradit.com

"Whatever our souls are made of, his and mine are the same."

Emily Brontë

STRENGTH

1
AMELIA

Amelia had to get out of the house. Specifically *this* house, which now felt like a macabre gallery of her past, every item narrating its own unique story to torture her.

It was her home. The setting for the fondest of her adult memories. But it also served as a constant reminder of everything she'd given up. Of Jacob. Of all the ways she tried to justify this crippling heartbreak, in an attempt to move on and start a new life without him.

If Jacob's memory—the light scent of his sweat, his goofy countenance and ringing laughter—wasn't haunting her thoughts, then the illuminated porch light across the street served as equal torment. Oz kept it on, hoping she would find her way across the street. *To talk,* he assured her, when he managed to grab her attention, as they were both rolling out garbage cans. *I need to talk about this with someone. With you. You're the only one who understands.* She'd made a point after that of managing her weekly refuse before Oz got home.

Months of him dancing through her dreams had left them both confused, desiring something they had no business even giving passing thought to. Meanwhile, her heart ached in the absence of the one man she'd ever loved, while Oz mourned the unexpected loss of his wife. Despite her skills as a counselor, and gifts as a Deschanel, conversation didn't beget resolution. Only more confounding misery.

"It's all so much. Too much. I can't fathom this loss. It's not real to me, not after everything she and I went through. But you, Amelia... you are so vivid. Alive. I can't... I won't... but I need to make sense of this. I love you, and God help me, I don't know how to turn off the emotions, and wanting, screaming through my every pore."

Amelia had tried as best she could to support Oz through his grief, until he said those words. "Oz, my mother explained this is an expected side-effect of extended dreamwalking. It will go away. And even if it doesn't—"

"Amelia, I can't eat! I can't sleep! I can't think about *anything* except how powerfully empty I feel when you're not around. When I close my eyes, I long to be in your mind again, where I can be close to you. I'm not in control of myself, and you're the only one I can make sense of this with!"

Amelia would never tell him she understood, even felt the same way. For whatever attachment—she refused to call it love—had formed in those months of dreamwalking, it wasn't *right.* Wasn't *okay.* And despite that it *felt* real, there was no way it could be. Had she known this could happen,

Amelia would've pushed him from her head the first time he showed up. Even if it meant her demise.

She slipped down into the old recliner, as Miss Kitty, her Siamese, hopped in her lap for affection with a happy, rumbling purr. Even her beloved cat reminded her of Jacob. They'd picked her out together, at the animal shelter in Metairie. It was Jacob who named her, declaring, *She has such a sassy look about her. You know when she introduces herself to other cats, she gets all puffed up and says, "That's MISS Kitty to you, pal."*

Tears threatened at every moment of every hour. Amelia's stomach refused food, and her body, having slept for nearly three months, insisted upon being conscious through every painstaking emotion. She had to fight it, to not give in. It was dangerous, and deadly. But she was so *tired.*

Something had to change, and only Amelia had the power to change it.

THE SOUND OF THE DOOR CHIME WOKE HER. MISS KITTY BOLTED for the door, something she only did when she was sure who was on the other side. *Jacob,* Amelia realized, taking a quick glance at the clock. Somehow, she'd lost several hours.

With a deep breath, she opened the door. Her heart stood before her, his disheveled look a mirror image of her own. "*Blanca,*" he greeted, in a low voice. He wouldn't meet her eyes, and she was grateful for it. The tenderness might have been enough to make her doubt the courage of her convictions. The comforting timbre of his voice was already distressing enough.

“Hi,” she replied, opening the door wider to allow him entrance. The second he stepped into the foyer, the room lit up with his presence, as if to say, *Ahh, this is more like it.* So did Amelia, though it wasn’t a feeling she could allow herself to linger in. “I was going to make some sweet tea, but I fell asleep. I have bottled water, though, if you’re thirsty.” *He knows there’s bottled water. He bought it.*

Though the sweat beaded at his brow from the sweltering August heat, Jacob shook his head. “Naw, I’m fine. Are you okay, Amelia? I mean, overall?”

Her heart surged again. Oh, how she longed to tell him, *No, I’m absolutely miserable without you. I’m lost. Devastated, and broken in ways I can never repair. Even breathing is too much sometimes.* But instead she said, “I’m holding up. My family needs me. Especially Ashley, now that Christine took the boys and ran off.”

Jacob shook his head. “I heard. Tell him... well, I mean, you don’t have to tell him. But I’m so sorry.”

“I’ll tell him,” Amelia promised. Jacob and her brother had always been fond of one another, despite having little in common. Ashley was as disappointed as Colleen when Amelia set her mind on a life without Jacob.

But neither of them understood what Amelia had been through, when her mind locked her in a prison for three months. None except Oz, and he was the last person on Earth she wanted to see.

“So... you said you had the rest of the boxes packed?” Jacob ventured, looking around the room in what seemed a mixture of awkwardness and longing.

“Oh! Yes, let me get them,” she answered, and started up the stairs, toward the room they’d shared for years. She was surprised to hear his steps following her, but she shouldn't have been. Always a gentleman, he never would have let her bring them all down on her own.

As they turned the corner into the room, his strong arms came around from behind, gently encircling her. His hot breath tickled her neck, as he entreated, "*Blanca... why*?"

Amelia stared straight ahead, rigid, though her heart raced as hard, if not harder, than his. "This was always the ending, Jacob. We just didn't know it."

"The only ending I ever envisioned was one with us growing old together, bickering over who was picking dinner," he teased, though his tone remained solemn. "Nothing you've said has convinced me that can't happen. I don't understand any of this, and I think it's because you don't, either."

It would hurt to face him in the middle of such a discussion, but Amelia couldn't say these things to a blank wall. She turned, and looked directly into his eyes. "You'll never know what I went through. Even if I tried to explain it, you will still never, ever know. And I wouldn't want you to." *For your sake.*

Jacob's lips tensed, a familiar attempt to conceal his emotions. "Is it Oz? If it is, I don't need the details. A nod will be sufficient."

"No," she replied, quickly. Maybe too quickly. "Absolutely not! It isn't like that." *Oh, but it was. Not by any choice I made, or would make, but still.*

"He saved your life, so I can't hate him for that, but when you woke, things between the two of you..." The undercurrent of his words held a dare to convince him he was wrong.

“It isn’t what you think,” Amelia reassured him. “We went through something unspeakable together. But I’ve never... would never...” Her voice choked up.

Jacob looked as if he might have a witty, cutting retort loaded, but his kindness overcame the harsh words. “I believe you.” His hand went up to touch her face, and for a moment, she closed her eyes and allowed the familiar comfort. “And you’re wrong.”

Amelia looked up. She couldn’t hide the tears, but it didn’t matter. She’d made no secret of her pain.

“The night you woke up, you said you’d destroyed me. That you’d sworn to give me a better life than the one my family left me with, but instead ruined it. You didn’t destroy me, Amelia.”

Now his other hand also held her face, as he kissed her trembling mouth. “You saved me.”

He left Amelia standing in stunned silence. It wasn’t until she heard the front door close that she realized he’d left without his boxes.

2

TRISTAN

Tristan didn't notice his elbow knock the old man's drink off the bar because he'd been too busy pouring out the sordid details of his life history. He didn't stop to think, not after the first drink, nor the tenth, that the man might not be interested in the drunken slurry of words and sentences Tristan haphazardly slung together in one long and incoherent narrative.

"Cursed," he spat, again, repeating himself with conviction. "Did I mention we're all cursed?"

The man nodded politely, glancing at his watch, but Tristan was far past the point of picking up on social cues. He continued rambling, oblivious. "Incest... and curses... and curses... and *death.*" He uttered the last with a lowered voice, studying the old man for the anticipated shock of such a revelation. The old man obliged.

The bartender leaned to pour Tristan another whiskey, but the old man gave her a subtle shake of his head. She stopped mid-pour, but Tristan lifted the empty glass anyway, wild-eyed and lost in his twisted memory. "They're all dead. All of them. My sister. My mother. My unborn child."

The old man clucked sympathetically, and Tristan took this, as he had all evening, as a sign to continue. "Mom was always nuts, but no one ever foresaw her offing herself. And how could I have known Emily was going to get an abortion? Is it my fault I didn't want to bring a cursed baby into the world? Married women make the worst girlfriends!"

Tristan slammed his still-empty glass down on the bar as the first real wave of dizziness washed over him. When his mother died months ago, he'd only just turned twenty-one. While generally responsible, other than his disastrous affair with Emily, he'd prided himself on mostly doing the right thing. But after his mom threw herself off the balcony of his uncle's plantation, Tristan Sullivan didn't have much interest in being a good kid anymore.

It had been the worst year of Tristan's life, following a lifetime of shitty years.

At first, it only took two drinks before the dizziness kicked in. Four before the bartender would politely suggest he find another establishment. Now, he was closing in on an even ten before the barkeep would make her requisite call to the cab company. She had his address on a notepad now, which was just as well, because Tristan could hardly be bothered to remember anything that didn't quell the pain.

"I'm very sorry about your family, son," the old man lamented, with a tinge of genuine sympathy. Though Tristan had allowed himself to imagine encouragement from the old man all night, it was not until this moment, this real human connection, that Tristan's emotions got the best of him.

The tears erupted, carving a waterfall of torture down his flushed cheeks. Tristan hated crying because once the waterworks started, there was little he could do to stop them, and he inevitably landed on the verge of an all-out hyperventilation fit. No better than the newbs he taunted in World of Warcraft when they pitched a tantrum over a lost loot roll.

"There, there, son," the old man consoled, softly patting Tristan's hand with his own weathered palm. For a fleeting moment, Tristan sensed familiarity of the man; this was someone he knew, but from where? "Let's get you a cab."

Tristan felt his belly turn over, all he'd eaten lurching forward in one unfortunate wave. "No," he managed to whisper, before emptying the contents of his stomach all over the kind man's lap.

The bartender rushed around to help clean up, but Tristan was already stumbling toward the door. Preoccupied with the sour mess, no one noticed as he ran into the wall, and then rolled into the wooden double doors, falling out into the street.

The humid Gulf air washed over Tristan in a rush, bringing him momentarily to his senses. He inhaled the soft scents, driving new air into his lungs. No sooner had this sensation brought him relief then it was taken away, as a fond memory surged up, bringing him back to reality.

Spring nights. Fishing with Dad on the Mississippi. The hum of cicadas. Measuring catfish. Savory scents of cayenne, garlic, and cornmeal, making his mouth water as they fried their catch outdoors in a weathered cast iron skillet.

Tristan's dad no longer took him fishing in the cool evenings. His father didn't do much of anything anymore, if it required reflexes more involved than staring blankly at the shadows on the wall. Connor Sullivan rode out a leave of absence from work that had the potential to be indefinite.

As a Deschanel there was no such thing as "normal," but that didn't mean Tristan had grown up without comforts. Before tragedy struck, he could almost ignore his mother's emotional absence, and his father's willful ignorance of her neglect. He could play with his sister, Danielle, and pretend their life was as amazing and colorful as his imagination would stretch. He knew his mother believed in the Curse, but his mother also still believed in the Tooth Fairy, most likely. So what did it matter to a kid like Tristan, who had the gift of seeing the world exactly as he wanted it to be?

You can never marry. Never have kids, she would say, like a broken record.

But you *did,* he insisted.

And I will pay the price for that sin.

Then his sister, Danielle, died. A victim of a hit-and-run driver, though to hear Tristan's mother tell it, she was a casualty of something much more sinister. *I told you I would pay the price,* she would lament to her son, through her tears and sorrow, unburdening feelings a child of Tristan's age should never be required to absorb. *This isn't about you,* he wanted to say, but by then his mother had drifted too far away to appreciate his wisdom.

Tristan's father had been a passable caregiver, though his disregard of his wife's condition was more harmful to his son than he realized. With the absence of a strong parental figure to guide him, Tristan ultimately raised himself.

That early maturity didn't mean he wasn't lonely, though; that he didn't crave the comfort found in the arms of someone who cared. It was almost no surprise he'd sought out older, married women. *They're safe,* he'd tell his cousin Amelia. *They won't want to marry me, or have children by me.*

But it's wrong, she would say, more worried than judgmental.

It's all I have.

He should have anticipated that, after a year of seeing Emily, one of them would fall for the other. As he grew beyond the initial comfort and into a steady pattern with her, he refused to acknowledge his inconveniently growing feelings. But nothing had caught him off-guard more than her pregnancy. Everything happened so fast... first, his mother's suicide. Then, Emily's secret abortion, happening while he was lost in grief over his mother's final choice. Finally, other loved ones falling around him as he struggled to process his increasing pain.

And, with this culmination of losses, Tristan's world crumbled. He didn't have the emotional fortitude, or the desire, to put it back together.

Tristan wasn't wearing a watch, but knew it was past two in the morning. Some of the bars that closed early had already turned off their lights, and only the few, resilient ones, kept going. He turned toward home, toward the Garden District, and then pivoted and wandered in the direction of the river instead.

He didn't know where he was going, only that he didn't want to go home.

Tristan slept through the morning and afternoon. Finally, a phone disturbed his drunken slumber.

The sound traveled across the room, from the pocket of his pants. He shoved the pillow over his head to drown out the shrill R2D2-esque beeping.

"Ain't you gonna get that?" a rough, female voice crowed from his left. Startled, he peeked out from under the pillow. A middle-aged blonde woman lay naked beneath the covers. A poorly maintained grin cracked her aging, over-tanned skin. Her thinning, brittle hair resembled a rat's nest. Tristan didn't recognize her, and as he took in the situation, he realized he didn't recognize the bed... the room... or anything else.

"Shit," he whispered, summarizing the numerous possibilities tumbling around in his brain. This wouldn't be the first time he'd woken in a strange place over the past couple of weeks. Last week, he found himself curled up on a park bench. A couple nights ago, he'd passed out in a ditch, covered with beads. But never in the bed of a woman he could not even remember *meeting*.

The woman let out a hacking cough, and lit a cigarette. Tristan's heart raced as he tried to reach for any memory, anything at all, to bridge the gap between his walk toward the river and his awakening in the bed of this strange woman. Meanwhile, the ringing stopped only to start anew.

"Whoever it is, they really wanna talk to ya," she said with another mucus-laden cough. Tristan cringed. He wanted to believe he had not *slept* with her, that his lack of memory meant nothing had happened. But he knew better. Tender cuts on his back slapped him with reality.

He slipped out of the bed, wrapping a blanket around his waist as he went for his pants. *Markus,* the caller ID said. He checked the clock next to the bed. Past four. Sighing, he answered.

"What?"

"I need to talk to you," Markus stated. His tone was firm and commanding, as always, but Tristan sensed something else beneath the surface. Something less confident.

"Well, I need a lot of things that I don't get," Tristan retorted.

"Tristan," Markus' voice was unsteady, "your father shouldn't be alone, and I need to go visit Katja and the twins."

"Oh, in that case, *fuck* no! Why am I my father's keeper, and not the other way around?" A tidal wave of awful emotions—first nausea, then regret, anger, loss, and finally despair—rushed over him as the image of the twins popped into his head. Of Katja. And Alain. Of all the pain, havoc, and mayhem they unleashed on their already-suffering family. "You should stay away from those devil-spawn, Mark."

Deep sigh. "You didn't come home last night after the bar. Where are you?"

"You're my cousin, not my mother," Tristan snapped, then gasped as he lost hold of the blanket. The woman purred as he scrambled to reclaim modesty. He cringed, gripping the blanket tighter, determined to win the resulting tug-of-war.

"I'm also your friend. I'm trying to help."

"Call one of the Sullivans, then, if you want to help. Let *them* deal with Connor."

"He's your father, Tristan. He's hurting, too."

Everything around Tristan abruptly felt painfully real, and there was a clarity about the situation he was in—this room, this woman, this debacle—that terrified him. *I need another drink...*

"I'm sorry... I can't," he stammered, and ended the call.

3
OZ

"Darling, if I'd known you were coming over tonight, I wouldn't have put them to bed so early," Oz's mother, Catherine, apologized. "But it's a school night and I hate to wake them."

Oz nodded mechanically, sinking into the leather recliner without a word. In the end, perhaps it wasn't such a bad thing, not seeing his kids. He didn't want to upset them, in his current frame of mind.

"Would you like to stay the night?" she added, evoking her ever-present need to protect and coddle her only child. "Rosaria can have your bed made up in no time. Oh, and I can make grillades and grits in the morning!"

Oz quickly shook his head. His mother's comfort only made him feel further connected to his guilt-laden grief. "I have an early day tomorrow. Need to close out some cases at the firm and finalize my leave of absence. I'll be back tomorrow afternoon to visit with Christian and Naomi when they're out of school."

Catherine's wide, concerned eyes followed him as he stood and moved to approach her for the requisite hug. Everything he did these days seemed more an automated response from his nervous system than a considered thought. "Okay darling," she replied, eyes still watching him with fearful disquiet. "You should say goodnight to Papa Colin, before you go. He's been asking about you since the service." When Oz opened his mouth with the predictable question, she explained, "Your grandfather's house is being renovated. He'll be in the guest house for a couple of weeks."

Oz could think of few things he desired less at that moment than socializing with family, but to refuse would mean causing his mother more worry, so he agreed and ventured toward the small cottage at the back of the property.

The pool house had long ago been remodeled to the status of full apartment, for reasons Oz could never understand as his parents insisted visitors stay in the main house when they visited. But it was ideal for his grandfather, who, at the age of seventy-five, was still as spry and independent as he'd ever been.

Oz knocked on the door. His grandfather answered almost immediately, wearing a silk bathrobe with the initials "CS" embossed at the breast in elegant gold script. Colin Sullivan Sr., more than most Sullivans, felt it important to let the world know all he had accomplished.

"It's about damn time," his grandfather chided, ushering him in with suspicious quickness.

Oz raised an eyebrow as his grandfather double bolted the door. "For?"

The older man clapped two firm hands on Oz's shoulders, giving him a searching look. "First, let me say once again how sorry I am about Adrienne. Truly, she was a fine woman." Before Oz could utter the same thank-you he'd come accustomed to offering over the past couple of weeks, his grandfather launched right into his next thought. "But, Colin, when I said at the service you needed to come see me, I didn't mean for you to take your time about it."

"I've been dealing with a lot, Papa," Oz replied, feeling like any defense in this case should be unnecessary.

Colin Sr. moved toward the mini bar, returning to a half-mixed drink he'd been preparing when Oz arrived. "Martini? Dry gin, of course." Oz shook his head, and watched his grandfather strain his own into the long-stemmed crystal.

"Oz, relax a moment," his grandfather gestured toward the velvet sectional. "We have some things to discuss, and while you may not be in the mood to spend quality time with your old grandpa, I'm going to insist you to indulge me."

"I need to be home in about an hour, Papa, but you have me until then." His eyes pointedly traveled up to the clock above the mantle, as he stifled an impolite yawn.

Colin Sullivan Sr. dropped all airs and leaned forward, his expression grave. "Dreamwalking. We used to call it 'night visiting' when I was your age, but what did we know? We never had a fancy group of sorcerers to catalogue it for us the way your wife's family did."

Oz's sleepiness disappeared in an instant. "Papa, what are you talking about? You know about dreamwalking?"

"Know about it?" Colin Sr. scoffed. "Bloody hell, I gave it to you! You think something like that happens randomly?"

Oz perched at full attention. "How *could* I have known

that, when no one told me? You never said a word, and my parents did everything they could to convince me it never happened."

"You can blame me for that, if you wish," his grandfather replied, sipping the martini before continuing. "Your father knew all about it, because I'd told him the horror story the night visitations brought upon my own young life. I wanted better for you. Had I known that meddlesome Deschanel woman was re-introducing these foolish notions, I would have stopped her myself!"

"Her daughter was *dying*," Oz replied. There were other things he could add. For example, that this same daughter was now constantly on his mind, despite having no business renting space there. That his love for her was, somehow, superseding the grief he should have felt over losing his wife.

That these unnatural feelings were slowly killing him, too.

Where Amelia was concerned, it felt as if his heart might burst when a thought of her crossed his mind. But as to his own grief, and his lost wife, he was so numb that if the ceiling caved in atop him, he wouldn't have flinched.

Colin Sr. shook his head slowly. "Might have been better off. You might both wish you were dead when it's all over."

"Forgive me, but I'm exhausted, so if you could please not speak in riddles..."

His grandfather sat up straight, cinching the silken belt at his waist. "Then let me speak absent riddles, young man. Dreamwalking ruined my life, and stole your grandmother's."

"Nana died of cancer," Oz reminded him.

"She *had* cancer, but she was dying from the moment she met me," Colin Sr. went on. "I'll start at the beginning and tell you a story that will conflict with the one you've come to know. But you're a grown man now, and there's no reason for me to lie to you. You understand that, don't you?"

Oz nodded, though he was beginning to wonder if his grandfather hadn't finally lost some of his marbles.

"I met your Nana Josephine when we were barely old enough to tie our own shoes, mind. I was five when I first saw her playing on her porch with her older sister, Darlene. I can't rightly tell you what drew me to her, but we were fast friends, the two of us. And the friendship grew as we moved from our learner years into high school.

"I never dreamed that one day I could love her, though perhaps I always did. But after I left for college, your nana was entering her senior year without me around, and she got involved with this scamp by the name of Alden Chalmers. Pretty boy, never been held accountable a day in his life. You know the type. And as much as I adored Jo, it's the truth to say he was way out of her league. I suspect he thought she'd be more apt to tolerate his ways if she felt he was too good for her.

"It didn't take long before Alden's jealous side came out, and it had a taste for violence. She didn't tell me about any of it, of course, because she knew I'd have killed him. But I found out anyway."

"How?" Oz asked.

"Your nana wasn't my only friend left in the school," his grandfather explained. "I came home for winter break and confronted her about it, and she broke down, thinking I was mad at her. I wasn't mad at her at all. I absolutely wanted to kill the scoundrel! But, she pleaded with me not to. She swore up and down she loved him, and wanted to make it work, and made me promise not to touch him. I lied to her, and tried to think up ways I could take the hooligan out and make it look like an accident. Eventually, I returned to college, but I wasn't about to let it go.

"But then the darnedest thing happened, Oz. Can you guess?"

"You found your way into her dreams," Oz solved dutifully.

"I sure did. Unlike you, mine never manifested at all in childhood, or any time before that. Of course, the first few times felt like accident or coincidence, until one day I received a letter from her asking me how I'd done it. I was stunned, mind you. I never in a million years believed the experience was real. But it was, and she recalled all the details the same as I had."

"Was she mad?"

"Not at all," Colin Sr. replied, lifting the glass for another sip. He smiled briefly. "To the contrary, she was tickled pink. Thought it was a real lark. She wanted me to keep visiting her, and so I did. I began looking forward to sleep so I could see her again, despite that I was physically across the country. Ultimately, it was less about wanting to see her, and more about needing to. No, I don't mean love, but I think you understand, from your own experiences, what I *do* mean. All the while, I had a friend watching Alden to make sure he stayed in line. And he did, until he started suspecting your nana was stepping out on him."

"With you?"

His grandfather nodded. "He had no idea what was

actually going on. But she began acting weird, never wanting to see him at night, keeping secrets. He put two and two together, but he was only half right."

"And he punished her for it?" Anger, one of the first real emotions he'd felt in weeks, rose up as Oz thought of someone harming his sweet grandmother.

"Not the way you imagine... ol' Alden decided the only way he'd ever control Josephine Bartleby was if the law handed him that power. And so he proposed."

Oz frowned. "She didn't accept, obviously."

"She did accept, Oz, and she married him, before she even turned eighteen," Colin Sr. replied, finishing his drink. "No, we didn't tell you. Your cousins don't know, either, so try not to look so offended. It was a dark part of our history, and one we'd just as soon see buried for good."

Oz glanced out the window across the room at the spreading storm clouds, no stranger to dark histories. "I'm not offended, but I don't see why no one told us. It isn't exactly rare for people to be married more than once."

"Aye, but it is rare for a woman to become a widow at eighteen because she murdered her husband with the pruning shears he got her for a wedding present."

Oz choked on his words. "She murdered him? Nana? My nana? The same woman who set up a pet hospital for strays, and let all the kids turn her backyard into a jungle gym?"

"She murdered him, all right," his grandfather answered evenly. "And I convinced her to do it."

"But... *why?*"

"Because I wasn't in my right mind anymore, and neither was she. The nightly visits had turned our friendship into an obsession. Even when one of us wanted to do something else, we were pulled toward meeting, like someone had attached a tether. I grew to love your grandmother, Oz, but I also grew to hate her. Yes… I hated her. And she hated me, for unintentionally forcing her to give up her free will. But we were stuck with each other, because we could no longer bear the pain of separation. It was either continue to fight what was happening, and die, or surrender to it and join our lives together."

"It's not like that with Amelia," Oz insisted. "I don't love her, or hate her. And anyway, it's over. She's okay now, and we haven't seen each other since… since everything fell apart."

Colin Sr. expressed his skepticism through a raised brow. "You turned it off? Just like that?"

No, far from it. "Yes," Oz lied. "Just like that."

His grandfather didn't hide his suspicion well. "Then keep it off, Oz. If you've managed to walk away, then you must be a stronger and finer man than I. I couldn't walk away from Josephine, despite knowing it was bad for both of us. I couldn't turn off the need. And she hated me all the rest of her life, blaming me for pulling her into a situation that was never her decision. She loved you and your cousins dearly, and of course her own four children, but her life behind the curtain was filled with misery. All because I didn't understand the ramifications of my compulsion."

Oz, please. I'm so very sorry for everything that's happened, and I wish I could comfort you, but we both know why I can't, Amelia had pleaded, nearly the same words on every trip he'd made back to her porch over the past weeks.

Amelia, only you understand what I'm going through. No one else knows what happened in there!

And don't you think that's for the best? We have to leave that time, and all the jumbled emotions, behind. If we don't, it will destroy us both.

Not being near you is destroying me now.

"I should get going, Papa," Oz said, rising with his words.

Colin Sr. moved to embrace him. "I'm so sorry again, about Adrienne," he breathed in his grandson's ear, clapping him on the back with both arms. "Life can be a real rancorous bitch sometimes."

"It's my children I'm most worried about," Oz mumbled, kissing his grandfather's wrinkled cheek. "But we'll get through it. The Sullivans are survivors."

"Family before all else," his grandfather replied. "And you know what Sullivan means, don't you?"

Oz sighed, smiling as he recalled how his grandfather often asked him this as a small child. "The steady hand to victory."

"Aye. We persist, and we triumph. We always have. As will you." Colin Sr. led him toward the door, opening it to the deep gray skies of a burgeoning thunderstorm. "But you might find ruin instead, if you pursue these dreams with the Deschanel girl. They'll distract you from what's important, and drown you both if left unchecked. You say you've moved on? Then move on, Oz, and never, ever look back."

Oz nodded obligingly and left.

EXPECTEDLY, SLEEP DIDN'T COME EASY THAT NIGHT FOR OZ, despite the physical and mental exhaustion that never seemed to give him peace.

It was a terrible feeling, to be grateful to your mother for taking care of your kids because you were incapable. Oz fought it initially, when Catherine insisted they take Christian and Naomi for a few weeks, or more. He was their *father* and they should be with him, he'd argued. But his father pointed out what his mother was too kind to say: Oz could barely be bothered to remember to shower in his current state, let alone feed and care for two young humans who needed more from him than ever before.

He loathed himself for the relief he felt when his mother came and picked up their things. But then the self-recrimination faded to the dull noise of a numbness he experienced only on the surface.

There were a lot of things Oz Sullivan should have been feeling following the unexpected death of his wife, but so far none of those sentiments had bothered showing up.

In fact, the only emotion which *had* emerged was the confused love he felt for Amelia after helping bring her out of her coma. It was the last thing in the world he wanted to be dealing with, but the only thing his mind was allowing him to spend time on. And, after speaking with his grandfather, he now had a better idea as to why.

Oz needed to talk to Amelia, and share what he'd learned. Together, they could make sense of their predicament. And maybe, just maybe, if he could do that, then whatever had turned him into a zombified version of himself might reverse and unwind the damage done.

After months of practice, he no longer needed to be at her side to slip into her dreams. He thought he might be able to do it from nearly anywhere. There were times when she remembered to block him from slipping through, but thankfully, tonight was not one of those nights.

Lying across the street from her, the connection was instant.

Before, he'd been entering a world constructed by her subconscious, resembling an alternate version of reality. Now that she'd emerged from her illness, entering her mind meant stepping into her actual dreams.

Oz found her immediately. Her near-white hair was piled above her head, woven with gaudy pink streamers. She was in her office—or what was her office, before she'd quit her job—counseling a patient.

That patient was Jacob.

"Why won't you let me mow your lawn?" Jacob demanded, his face beet-red. "I've been cutting it for years, and it's always been done to your liking!"

"It's too late for my lawn," Amelia lamented, shaking her tasseled head.

"It's never too late for lawn care, if you seriously care for your foliage," Jacob replied sadly.

Amelia wearily raised her head, preparing another rebuttal, when her eyes fell on the intruder in her dream. As realization pulled her forward, the dream façade faded, Jacob disappeared, the pink tassels fell away, and the office looked as it once had, in the real world.

"What are you doing here?" she demanded, shoving herself up and away from her desk. "Oz, you can't just show up in my head whenever you feel like it!"

Oz put his hands forward in defense. "I'm sorry. I am. But you won't talk to me when I come over, Amelia, and I'm going completely mad! I have so many thoughts rolling around in my head I can't make sense of, and the one person who might understand wants nothing to do with me!"

Wrath swirled through her expression as her mouth flew open, when Oz stepped toward her, placing a hand gently on her shoulder. "That didn't come out the way I intended. I know why you don't want to see me."

She averted her eyes, but didn't move away. "I get it, its confusing," she admitted, calming. "Olivia keeps trying to tell me it's my mother's fault, for pushing you into my head. That Mom knew the risks and did it anyway. But what does it matter, whose fault it is? It's done, and I'm alive, and I'm grateful. But the life I came back to isn't the one I left behind."

"For either of us," Oz agreed, closing the gap between them. Even in her dreams, her skin carried the soft scent of morning dew. He restrained the urge to breathe in deeply. "I know how I feel. I don't know why, but I know it's real."

"Oz..."

He wasn't aware, until that very moment, that he didn't intend to tell her what his grandfather had conveyed. At least not yet. "It's painful to be apart from you. An ache that won't go away. You can't tell me I'm the only one."

Amelia watched him with sad, tired eyes. "That's why you can't be here. Neither of us felt anything for each other beyond friendship until the dreamwalking. Right now, the residual effects from that are still lingering, but all things fade. This *will* fade, but until then, we each need to focus on our own lives."

"It won't," Oz insisted, stubbornly. He realized his grandfather's story might provide more structure for his argument. But the news could equally backfire, and he had things he desperately wanted to say. "It feels like there's constantly a part of me missing."

Amelia backed away. Her eyes were guarded, but her body language conveyed wariness. As if she thought he might throw himself at her. "That's the loss of Adrienne you're feeling."

"I *don't* feel it!" Oz cried, throwing his hands up. "That's the problem! I loved her with all my goddamn heart, but I feel *nothing* when I think of her death! Nothing! The only emotion my heart is letting me feel right now is this senseless, bewildering love I have for *you*!"

Amelia's expression softened, but she made no move to return to where he stood. "Oz, I won't try to feed you a bunch of therapist babble about how everyone grieves differently, and that what you're feeling is normal. This isn't your first time as a widower. But what happened with you and me is confusing already complicated matters, and even more reason for you to focus on things at home."

"I want to, but I can't," Oz told her. His voice cracked, and his chest was heavy. "I'm losing it, Amelia. I honestly am. And I need you."

These words, finally, were what appealed to her kind and helpful nature. Once her soft lips landed on his forehead, he could no longer hold the tears back. "We can talk here," she sighed, reluctantly. "But nowhere else. And only for a short time... until we can figure out how to move forward."

Oz raised his bleary eyes to look upon her face, but she was gone.

4
JACOB

Jacob sat on his lopsided balcony, overlooking the river. Ahead, the Steamboat Natchez slowly eased back into port for the evening. Beneath, the loud sounds of proletarian commerce, police sirens, and crimes not-yet-committed filled the air.

He could have afforded better, but there was a peacefulness about returning to the raucous and lively Irish Channel. His years there were not the happiest, by any stretch, but they remained the backdrop for a period of greater control than he currently possessed.

At the tender age of ten years old, Jacob had been handed off to Sister Agnes at Saint Louise Parochial Academy, after his last living relative in Ireland decided he was too much of a burden. First pulled from the safety of his family's arms, then from the country of his upbringing. *Our orphanages are overflowing with wee brats n'one wants. Ye'll get better care fro' th' one Father O'Connor recommends in the states,* were the closest to tender words Jacob would ever get from his aunt.

For most coming through the doors of Saint Louise, it was an expensive Catholic school, but for the few, unfortunate children without family, like Jacob, it was also an orphanage, with none of the accouterments of the school itself.

"Ye poor, sweet dear," Sister Agnes had lamented, eyeing his torn clothes and lack of luggage. "Keep yer nose down and focus on yer studies and you'll be fine, lad." But he didn't miss how she looked away as the words floated off her lips. Not the first unfortunate orphan who'd passed through, apparently. It didn't take much to guess how their tenure had ended.

He quickly discovered the difference between the orphans and students at St. Louise was bigger than where each rested their heads at night. The academy was largely funded by some of the wealthier Uptown families—including the Deschanels, though Jacob wouldn't learn that until much later—some of whose children were students. Allowing housing for orphans made it possible for those same benefactors to increase their charitable tax deductions.

The sisters were understandably terrified of angering their source of support, and so what passed for structure and discipline at St. Louise was nothing more than gentle scolding, unless you were one of the orphans, in which case martyrdom was an achievable goal.

Nearing adolescence when he arrived, it was painfully evident from the beginning that Jacob's chances of finding a family were slim. And it didn't take long for the other children to figure out why Jacob had been shipped all the way from Ireland, alone and with nothing to his name.

Jacob came to know his bullies by their features, rather than their names, a trick his father taught him. *Don' see yer aggressor as a person, Jacob. It softens yer heart, and exposes yer weaknesses. Reduce them to naught more tha' a word that makes them nothin'.*

The worst of the bullies was an overweight redhead, with freckles so dense they seemed as if they might eventually swallow up his eyes. Jacob thought of him as Speck.

About a month after Jacob showed up, Speck tore the Saint Jude medal from Jacob's neck; a gift from his mother. "Your dad musta prayed to Jude about what a lost cause his family was!'" Speck's group of buddies rallied around him, ready to nod and give agreement. "Way I see it, you're already dead, you dirty mick. Killing you would be doing God a favor."

"I don' know wha' God ye pray to, but mine doe'nt require favors," Jacob replied, already squaring his stance, as Pa showed him. Ready.

"Take the cock out of your mouth and try that again," Speck cracked, and his friends roared. It wouldn't be the last time they ridiculed his rural Irish brogue, but Jacob would be sure they remembered the first.

"I suggested th' same thing to yer ma last night, but she was enjoyin' herself too much to heed th' advice," Jacob quipped back.

Speck threw the first punch.

Jacob's father had been an amateur pugilist back in Ireland, supplementing his unreliable income with fights several nights a week. And while he granted little time for his children, he spent what he did have teaching Jacob and his brother, Enoch, how to fight.

Yer stance is everything. Only let him hit ye for misdirection. Next most important is knowin' yer opponent. Yah fightin' a big boy? Wear him out. Then strike when he's winded.

Over time, Jacob would fill out, but as a child he was small and wiry; an easy target. But no target was easy while moving, and so Jacob danced and dodged until Speck coughed and wheezed, all the while taunting his apparent lack of courage. And then Jacob waylaid the bigger boy with blows that would have made Liam Donnelly proud.

It took several of Speck's friends, and Sister Agnes, to stop him, and Jacob was still swinging when they hauled him away. No one was surprised when Speck was given comfort, and Jacob solitary detention.

Sister Agnes came to see him in punishment, to tend to his split lip. "Jacob, don't ye know you're the best o' the lot? This is no way to go through life."

Jacob had looked up, grinning through a mouthful of blood. "But I won, Sister."

She shook her head with a heavy sadness. "Tis not a victory if it comes at the cost of yer soul."

"Then there's no use in talkin' about it, Sister, 'coz my Pa a'ready took my soul when he dragged my family wit' 'im to hell."

The match with Speck marked the beginning of Jacob Donnelly fighting his way through his studies. Over time, only the bravest, and boldest, dared take him on.

But as he came of age in Saint Louise's, and he received fewer challenges, Jacob slowly came to the awareness he wasn't fighting for self-defense anymore, but to reclaim something critical he'd lost. His soul, perhaps. And the longer he went without a fight, the worse his studies fared. His knuckles ached, and his shoulders itched.

When he reached the age of fourteen—the cutoff for Saint Louise—he was sent to a sister private school in Uptown, where fighting meant immediate expulsion. But the loss of Sister Agnes, and her constant steadying, hurt almost as much as losing his physical outlet.

Sister Agnes, as it turned out, was from an Irish village not far from where the Donnellys met their gruesome end. For this reason, and many others, she had a soft spot for Jacob the moment he walked through the venerable doors of Saint Louise. Her Pa was also a fighter, and she recognized the hunger, and need, in Jacob's eyes all too well. She seemed to understand telling him to stop would be like asking him not to breathe. And so, she introduced him to a young Russian who ran a fight club on the river.

Vasily was not much older than Jacob, but his face bore the tale of a full life already lived. He immediately witnessed the fire in Jacob, but cautioned him he would find fighting with Russians a completely different experience. While naturally lean like Jacob, they spent their days and nights in the gym, building muscle mass and pushing themselves far beyond their natural limit. For Jacob, fighting was a release. For them, a way of life.

They called themselves the Kremlin, an ironic jab at the government they'd eagerly left behind.

In the beginning, Jacob lost nearly all his bouts. The Russians laughed, wheedling him to go back to his school and fight little kids. This didn't deter him in the slightest. He walked away with broken ribs, cracked jaws, and eventually got used to seeing through one eye at a time. Sheer Irish stubbornness meant he worked harder, and started training with Vasily, who, impressed by Jacob's determination, took him personally under his wing. He learned to be an effective southpaw outside fighter, discovering a way to blend technique and instinct. He "had a chin," as Vasily would say, a fighter who could take the big hit and find the inner resolve to remain standing. And eventually, he started winning.

He became known as "Fightin' Irish" amongst the Kremlin, and when they opened up private matches with other fight clubs around the greater New Orleans area, they always pitted him against the biggest opponents. A pugilist remake of David and Goliath, Jacob could dance around them for untold time, wearing them down, before going in for the victory. Though he hit his growth spurt as a sophomore in high school—shooting up to over six feet—it didn't dull his quickness, or gift at reading opponents.

For the first time since his father murdered his family, he'd been alive with purpose.

But Jacob never mistook the satisfaction he drew from fighting with happiness. He'd long ago given up hope of ever finding *that.* Fighting was surviving.

When he was fifteen, Sister Agnes formally adopted him, retiring from her post at Saint Louise to tend to his care. And each night, when he came home, she'd be awake, ready to tend his wounds, and help him with his homework.

It was Sister Agnes who followed the Deschanel tragedies, and piqued Jacob's interest in the subject. Thanks to scholarships, and a modest trust fund established upon her retirement, she paid for his higher education at Tulane, seeing him securely ensconced on campus before returning to her own family in Ireland. And so Jacob had her to thank for not only helping him first find his control, but then paving the way for him to meet the one person who could make him forget about boxing altogether. The scars on his hands healed, just as the one on his chest, where his father's bullet had pierced. His heart burst with the recognition of what it meant to finally discover a means of being whole.

But Amelia was gone now, and with every day that passed, it grew increasingly doubtful she was ever coming back.

And once again, Jacob felt the ache in his knuckles, and the itch in his shoulders.

THOUGH JACOB HAD BEEN OUT OF THE FIGHT SCENE FOR NEARLY A decade, he'd kept in touch with Vasily, who'd since retired from the ring, but still checked in on the old crew from time to time.

There's a new club in Algiers, Vasily said. *New crew. New rules. But they'll take a man they don't know, if you catch my meaning. If you're having a rough patch, they won't ask questions.*

Jacob paused outside the doors of the unmarked bar with hesitation. Once he stepped through, he might never be able to turn back. Embracing this old release was his equivalent of accepting all hope was lost.

"Abandon all hope, ye who enter here!" a familiar voice externalized his feelings. Jacob whipped his head up to see a man tottering for balance, clutching a piece of paper he flapped belligerently in greeting. Over the exhaust, Jacob smelled the rancid liquor on his breath, wafting up on the artificial breeze from passing traffic.

"Tristan, what are you *doing* here?"

"Signing up to get my ass kicked, I hope?" Tristan grinned, stumbling against the building. Under the awning lights, Jacob was granted a clear view of the younger man's face, which boasted a split lip and developing black eye. "Oh, the other guy looks worse, trust me. Who do you think gave me the address?"

"You shouldn't be here," Jacob muttered, casting a searching glance at the old building, before reluctantly turning back to Amelia's cousin. He sighed, understanding Tristan was reading his thoughts. He'd been too distracted to stop him. "This place is bad news, Tris."

Tristan scoffed, kicking at a piece of upturned sidewalk. "You're here. Can't be that bad if the Prodigal Son of Ireland is a patron."

"I'm not a patron, and there's a lot you don't know about me," Jacob countered, slipping a hand over Tristan's shoulders. The latter stumbled into the embrace as he tried to move away, but then erupted with laughter, nearly knocking them both over.

"I know you're a pathetic son-of-a-bitch for letting Amelia walk away like that," Tristan replied. His words were so slurred that "son-of-a-bitch" came out more like "splunchsbish," but Jacob got the gist. "But I can't talk, I guess. I let my pregnant girlfriend kill our baby, so I suppose that makes me a pathetic son-of-a-bitch, too."

"Amelia has a right to her choices," Jacob started, then frowned. Reasoning would be lost on Tristan, so instead Jacob eased him down the dark alley, toward his parked car.

He fully expected Tristan to put up a fight, but instead the young man crumpled into a heap in the front seat, whimpering against the window.

As Jacob struggled to secure the passenger seatbelt, he told himself, *Tomorrow. I'll come back tomorrow.*

CONNOR THANKED HIM WHEN HE PULLED UP TO THE SULLIVAN house, explaining through his exhaustion how Tristan had been troubled since Elizabeth died, and how he felt helpless to stop his destructive behaviors.

But all Jacob could think of was the disturbed young boy he'd been when he came to Saint Louise, eyes wide, ready to fight the first person who dared say a word about him or his family. He didn't have a father to guide him, and keep him safe. But Tristan did.

"You can thank me by giving him the support he needs," Jacob replied, out the passenger window. "Tristan is a good boy, but he needs you to show him how to be a man."

Connor looked stricken, but his expression faded to benign acceptance, and he nodded.

Jacob pulled away, beleaguered by sadness at realizing Tristan fell into the same category as the rest of Amelia's family. People he once cared about as his own clan.

Now they were simply people he knew.

5
AMELIA

"Mia, you look exhausted," Ashley noted, handing her a fresh mug of coffee with chicory. "Mom said you need to keep focused on positive things right now."

Amelia accepted the warm drink with a grateful smile. "Mom says a lot of things," she replied, taking a deep sip. *And conveniently omits others,* she didn't add.

Ashley nodded. They drank their coffee together in silence.

He'd moved in temporarily, after Christine ran off with the kids. She'd been warning him of her intentions, but no one really expected her to follow-through on such a cruel threat. She and Ashley were both suffering from loss. But in her suffering she'd become someone else entirely.

Amelia couldn't blame Ashley for not wanting to be alone in his house, and her own circumstances left her longing for familiarity.

A glum silence overtook the siblings, as they shared their

misery, but neither attempted real conversation. *Look at us. The remaining Jameson kids, irreparably broken. Where did things go so horribly wrong?*

Though Ashley was the youngest, Amelia had always looked to him as the guiding star amongst the siblings: responsible, balanced. He'd never been susceptible to the family worries, or the fear mongering around the Curse. His presence comforted others in a way that said, *It's okay. Ashley is here.* But as she observed her baby brother's somber expression, and the stubble he'd not bothered to shave in weeks, she understood he'd reached his tipping point. The first of his strength departed when his daughter, Katey, died. The rest, when Christine took the boys and disappeared without a trace.

Amelia wanted to reassure him with the usual overtures. *She'll come back. She's just hurting, is all. Once she comes to her senses, she'll return.* But she wasn't so sure. Christine's anger toward Ashley after Katey died was venomous. She held her husband and his "nefarious family" culpable.

"I'm going to take those boxes to Jacob this morning," Ashley offered, as he finished his coffee. "Any message you'd like me to pass along?" The last question rang with misplaced hopefulness.

Amelia shook her head. "Thank you. The last time I saw him... well, I don't know if I could do it again."

He stood and kissed her forehead. "You know my feelings. But first and foremost, you're my sister, Mia. Your emotional health is a matter of life and death."

She reached a hand up and patted his face, as they drew comfort from each other.

• • •

Amelia didn't realize she'd dozed off until she found herself sitting in a cafe across from Oz. But the cafe floated on the river, green and pulsing with a lively tidal current. The sky above shone pink, with all the vibrant hues of cotton candy.

"Oz," she allowed, immediately steeling her emotional defense, "when I said we could meet here, I didn't mean all the time."

"I know. But this isn't about us. I promise," he assured quickly.

His momentary silence searched for her approval, but she said nothing, and he went on. "I woke up this morning and couldn't breathe. My first thought was a heart attack, but I decided more likely a panic attack. I used to get them after Adrienne had her accident, for those years until we found her and... I'm sorry. I should be asking before barging into your head. Is it okay?"

Amelia slowly nodded, internalizing the sigh forming. "This time." The scenery shifted to something more comfortable: her living room. Oz stumbled to the couch with a wistful air, and then heaved a deep sigh.

"She's really gone... isn't she? This isn't like before," he inhaled.

Carefully, Amelia took the seat across from him, unsure of the words he needed to hear.

"What kind of person am I..." His struggle for air halted his words. Amelia didn't want to be invasive, but she felt the rest anyway: *What kind of person feels relief when their wife passes?*

"A person filled with a thousand emotions that are

rightfully yours," Amelia soothed. "Adrienne was never the same after her accident. That affected you both."

"A part of her died in that car," Oz replied thoughtfully, as he gazed toward the stairs. Amelia couldn't tell who his words were directed at, but he had the faraway look of someone deep in remembrance. "She tried so hard to be the old Adrienne. But even when her memory came back, there was something... missing."

Amelia watched him, listening. Words were not what Oz needed. They would solve nothing. They would not bring Adrienne back, nor would they assuage his guilty conscience. Worse, they wouldn't explain why wrapping her fingers through Oz's felt natural. Why his subtle returned squeeze reminded her of an old, comfortable memory.

But it wasn't normal, or natural. Oz was grieving the death of his wife. Amelia, mourning the loss of the love of her life. *Jacob. He reminds me so much of Jacob, and it's only adding to this mountain of confusion.* "Oz, I'm going to call Nicolas to come stay with you for a couple days," she said, gently removing her hand from his. "You can help each other through this. And I don't think you should be alone." *Nor am I the right person to help.*

Oz didn't seem to hear her. "How do I explain this to the kids? To Christian?" He shook his head with a stunted, bitter laugh. "They don't grasp Adrienne isn't coming back. How do I tell Naomi she's lost her mother for a second time? I'm terrified for them."

Amelia considered her words carefully. "As an empath, I can take some of that from them," she began, tentatively. This was a dangerous offer. Grieving was an important part of the healing process, and taking the pain from others was a great risk to her, a lesson she'd nearly learned with her life. But perhaps this would help redirect Oz toward his family. "I can give them some peace."

Oz looked up at her. How had she never noticed his big, beautiful green eyes, how alike they were to Jacob's? "Will it… do you think… is it the right thing to do?"

"To take it all, no," she responded. "Enough to help them sleep at night, and avoid the nightmares, perhaps. Just enough they won't repress pain and let it eat them alive later. As their father, only you can make that decision." Her mother would kill her if she knew she'd offered such a thing, after what happened.

Oz stared at his hands, now folded tightly in his lap. She could sense so much from him that it overwhelmed her: his pain for the children, his hatred of himself. His desire for her companionship, and fear she might leave him alone.

"I don't want Nic, Amelia. The only moments of peace I know are when I'm with you."

Unconsciously, through an instinct which was still new to her, and very fresh, she rested her hand atop his. Under her touch, he again relaxed. "I'll help you," she assured, despite her objections, and her own misgivings. Despite her vast confusion over these feelings she couldn't explain, and wished would go away. Despite her heart's keen ache over her own loss.

Oz looked up and smiled through his bleary tears. "Thank you."

In the silence between them hung an awkwardness, which both of them understood but neither could quite define. It was the sensation of a comfort that didn't belong, but was not altogether unwelcome. The discomfiture of discovering you've loved the person sitting in front of you your whole life, and never known it.

But, mostly, it was fear of these realizations.

"Let's go see the children," Amelia decided.

LATER THAT EVENING, AMELIA AWOKE TO ASHLEY SITTING AT HER bedside, his face flushed with concern. "You're sick again," he observed, laying the back of his hand against her forehead. "What happened?"

"I helped Oz's children today," she admitted, wincing as she pulled herself to a sitting position. Her body felt weighted with lead. Disoriented, the way she felt after stepping off a boat. But she was stronger since her months of imperilment, her emotional muscles growing tougher with use. She would recover quickly. This time.

Ashley's eyes narrowed. In his expression she witnessed an ire so uncommon it took her breath away. A small wind gathered in the center of the room. "He needs to leave you alone, Mia."

Amelia was too tired to disagree. Her thoughts were dark with the confused grief of Naomi and Christian. It would pass, but for now, her body required rest.

She closed her eyes again, praying her dreams would be uneventful.

THE BONFIRE ROARED, FINGERS OF FLAMES REACHING FAR INTO THE clear sky, nearly tickling the bowing yew branches. Clean forest scents of damp soil and sweet aspen blended perfectly with the remains of roasted venison.

Beside her, Cianán yawned, brushing her long white braid aside with a tender smile before nudging the bottom embers with a thick charred branch.

They were old now. Their ages far beyond what they'd ever dreamed of reaching. She could find no complaint with the beauty in the life they'd shared together. The adventures. The passion. The bond that would last for all of time, thanks to the goddess' blessing.

Would she have been content with a single lifetime by Cianán's side? It mattered not, for this was their fate, and it could not be broken.

But glancing at him now... only hints of the black beautiful hair, lines around his eyes and mouth, weary eyes... she knew the answer was no. She welcomed, with an open heart, the comfort of knowing she would meet him in the next life.

"Cerridwen," he whispered, as he poured sand over the fire. Ever respectful of the nature of which they were birthed, of which they were critically intertwined, he would not leave a fire untended in their absence. "It is time."

Cerridwen's heart surged, her breath escaping in one powerful gasp. She'd been prepared for this moment. Stronger than this weakness bubbling up! It did not stop her from grasping Cianán's hand tight, and pulling it up to her still-beating heart.

He transferred some of his strength to her as he whispered, "Síoraíocht, a stór." *Eternity, my dearest.*

She nodded, leaning her head against his chest as his slowing heartbeat lulled her into the old comfort, in these, their final moments of this lifetime.

Closing her eyes, Cerridwen prepared to meet him in the next.

. . .

AMELIA AWOKE WITH A GASP SO POWERFUL IT SHOT HER STRAIGHT up in bed. She forced herself to take in the details of her room... the floral engraving in her bureau, the old plaster arches above her window frames, her red robe draped over the vanity bench.

Home, you're home.

Reclaiming some of her control, she pieced together the flashes from her dream. The old man with Jacob's eyes and smile. A snapshot in time lacking visible markers, but carrying the distinct feel of a place which could deservedly be referred to as ancient.

Her mind often found ways to incorporate Jacob into her dreams. But this was no ordinary nocturnal assembly. Some time had passed since her last seer's vision, but she recognized the tingling sensations traveling through her arms and legs, and the other, smaller, telltale signs, which were all present.

Yet this image was quite clearly from a time long past. She'd never had a recognitive vision, though she'd heard of others, like Aunt Elizabeth, who could summon them on occasion. Why she would have her first now was a mystery.

The one and only thing Amelia was sure of was that her seer's ability only came in her times of need. And her need had never been greater.

Interpretation, though, was dangerous. Prophecy was not her strength, and an attempt to make sense of something without proper experience could lead to the creation of problems worse than those she currently faced.

The safest option—her only option—would be to allow the visions to unfold on their own schedule.

6

TRISTAN

Tristan stumbled through the front door of the house he'd grown up in. He thought he'd slept off all the alcohol in his system, at the apartment of *another* strange woman, but strangely felt as drunk as he had when stumbling out of the bar the night before. His head throbbed, pulse thumped. With his father off in la-la land, and Markus visiting Katja again, Tristan was, for once, happy he didn't have anyone to answer to.

"Where have you been?" His father's voice, low and deep, startled him. Instead of staring at the wall, lost in his thoughts, Connor clutched a piece of paper, looking more lucid than Tristan had seen him in months.

"Does it matter?" Tristan retorted, rejoining his thoughts to his senses. Any happiness he had at seeing his dad clear-headed was overshadowed by annoyance. He would choose *now,* when Tristan only wanted to crawl in his bed and shut out the world, to step up and show concern. *Where were you when I needed you?*

"Don't get smart. I'm not your mother."

"It's nice you've decided to make an appearance and all, but I'm fucking exhausted," Tristan declared, and started toward his room.

"When were you going to tell me you got a DWI?"

Tristan stopped at the foot of the bannister. *Well, now I know what's on the paper.* Tristan didn't want to have this conversation with his father.

"Well, I haven't driven in two weeks, so that might've been your first clue," Tristan snapped. He didn't add the officer had reduced the offense upon realizing Tristan was a Deschanel. The ticket was severe enough, without reckless operation added.

"I should hope not!" his father bristled. "We're going to get you enrolled in classes first thing in the morning. And... treatment."

This peaked Tristan's attention. "Excuse me?" His hand slipped off the creaky railing and he marched toward the living room, where his father sat. "You haven't given a shit about me in months, and *now* you wanna play house? Sorry, not interested."

Connor stood, setting the folded letter on the mantle. "We both deal with grief differently. I'm sorry I haven't given you more of myself while you were dealing with your pain."

Tristan snorted. "I'm glad you've had the luxury of dealing with it your own way, *Dad.*"

"Be as angry with me as you want, Tristan, but we're putting you in rehab tomorrow. You may be an adult, but you're living under my roof."

Tristan's pulse quickened. The heat rose to his face so

fast he was overcome with a brand new wave of nausea. Though he wasn't allowed to mind read in the house, he was beyond any concern for the rules. He zeroed in on his father. *God help us, he's going down the same path as Elizabeth. Why didn't she tell me about this? I don't know how to help him. I love him so much. This isn't the life I wanted for our family.*

"Fuck you for caring now!" Tristan yelled. He reached past his father and snatched the legal notice off the fireplace, ripping it up in front of his face. The shreds of paper flitted to the ground, settling around their feet in messy piles. "If you really gave a shit you would have been there for me when I *actually needed you!*"

"You're going to rehab tomorrow," his father asserted. "And that's final."

"No, *that* is a bunch of bullshit, just like this faux parenting. It won't last. It'll be gone tomorrow." *What if it isn't? What if he really puts me in rehab?* He didn't need rehab. He needed normalcy. He needed his mother back. He needed to be part of a different family.

But Tristan couldn't have any of those things, and so escape gave him his only solace. What, really, was so wrong with that? Could anyone blame him? How was his retreat different from his father's?

"You were always such an easy child," his father said, with a whimsical smile. Tristan hated him in that moment. *Yes, I was easy because I never forced you to get through to Mom and wake her up. I raised myself.*

"I'm not doing this with you right now," Tristan asserted. He turned toward the door, realizing he couldn't stay. He needed to get out; to get away. His eyes caught sight of the key rack, where his car keys had been hanging since he was booked for the DWI. *A suspended license is only suspended if you get caught driving.*

"Don't even think about it," his father warned, but Tristan was out the door and sprinting to the car before his father could move from his corner.

CONNOR DIDN'T FOLLOW, BUT TRISTAN HADN'T EXPECTED HIM TO. Whatever had crawled up his father's ass, it was only temporary. He'd be back to his usual, melancholic self in no time.

At what point had his feelings for his father changed from vague annoyance to outright aversion? Connor had always been a decent man, and *just enough* of a father to make up for their lack of a mother, to ensure they were always taken care of. That they didn't starve, and their world continued to spin on its wobbly axis day in, and day out. But his father had a weak constitution, and Tristan guessed Connor imagined he was a better father than he actually was. He could afford himself this illusion because there were others who *did* take care of Tristan, and so his life's outward appearance was far more normal than the one behind closed doors.

It was Aunt Colleen who took him clothes shopping every year, so he didn't have to show up to the first day of school in ill-fitting pants or shirts. She would pick him up once a month to take him for a haircut, and usher him to his twice-yearly dental appointments. If Tristan was running a fever, he didn't go to his parents. He called his aunt, who would come, quietly, and lay her soft, healing hands on the sides of his head, quelling his illnesses. More than once, he guiltily wished Colleen was his mother, instead of the crazy, unstable Elizabeth.

Because of this bond, he'd grown up thinking of Amelia as his sister. Tristan's real sister, Danielle, had been too "cool" to hang out with him, as older sisters often were. But Amelia, eight years his senior, took him under her wing and included him in everything. Amelia and her brother Ben took him everywhere with them, and sometimes Tristan forgot they weren't really siblings.

But Ben was gone now, just as Dani was. Just as Tristan's mother was. Victims of that senseless, unjust Curse. Amelia had her own issues to deal with now, between the loss of Jacob and Ashley's family going AWOL.

That left only Markus on the list of people Tristan could count on. Markus, too, had plenty to consume him, but he chose to instead be Tristan's backbone, when he couldn't find his own.

Tristan's heart raced with shame as he sped down St. Charles, toward the Quarter. Markus should be with his sister, Katja, helping her recover. Instead, he was spending his evenings playing cat-and-mouse with Tristan, as he jumped from one bar to another, drowning his pain. Markus' illusions were quite good, and so Tristan humored him, but he needed to be more diligent about guarding his thoughts.

I need a drink. I don't want to think about Markus, or my father, or any of it...

7
COLLEEN

A light breeze passed through The Gardens, offering the first relief of the day. Colleen gracefully sipped her mint julep, while her sister, Evangeline, held hers pressed against her forehead in evident misery.

"You grew up here, Evie. Have you forgotten?" Colleen teased.

"Repressed memories!" Evangeline cried, setting the tall glass down. She switched to her handheld fan, ruffling her striped cotton blouse, currently unbuttoned to a level which would've been indecent had their location been less private. "Sweden and Washington have both done wonders toward helping me forget these unconscionable summers."

The bright colors of spring had faded to the earthy blooms of summer, as lively frogs and crickets sang in the subtropical heat. The crepe myrtle drooped languidly over the rectangular pool, which even Colleen had to admit looked like a refreshing escape.

Yet physical relief would not dull the emotional storm

brewing at the center of the Deschanel clan. Nearly two weeks had passed since the Curse claimed a victim, but the unpredictability of the blight had always been the most terrifying aspect.

Colleen was afraid to voice this hopefulness out loud, but her gut told her the storm had passed. For now. History proved the Curse was as capricious as it was malignant.

"Tell me once more, how did Katja became involved with Olivia?" Colleen probed. "I'm still struggling to understand this dynamic."

Evangeline waved the small fan before her face. "I've told you, the logic escapes me. Kat told us Olivia was being difficult, refusing to talk to her or Alain. Then, the world falls apart, and Kat turns to the person who was the least supportive."

"The accident" had turned into the safest way to refer to Alain's complete breakdown, which resulted in his self-inflicted death, the loss of one of his unborn children, and Katja's spine shattered. "Well, what does Maureen say?" Colleen pushed, though she knew the answer.

"Maureen speaks with no one. Not even Olivia. *Especially* Olivia, now that she's harboring Katja in her home, and going against her wishes. Maureen has always been spiteful, but how can she, after all we've lost and all that's happened, hate her own niece?"

Colleen sighed. "Any answer on my part would be pure conjecture. But Katja's defection of you and Johan... and Markus... now *that* is perplexing."

Evangeline's gaze traveled to an open spot in the yard, where Colleen's cats chased each other around a large, sculpted fountain, decorated with cherubs and various avian species. "If Olivia can provide her comfort, and help with the twins, then I can accept that. I only want her to be okay, Leena."

"And what does that even mean, for a Deschanel anymore?" Colleen replied as Cocoa hopped in her lap, with a gentle purr. "Despite Olivia's foibles, her heart is good, and she has a strong maternal instinct. Had she been raised by someone other than Maureen, things could've been very different for her. I've no doubt she will take care of Katja and the babies. I know that only gives you a small measure of comfort, though. I find myself experiencing similar fears over the well-being of my own children."

"Well, Ashley's situation will resolve itself soon, I'm sure," Evangeline replied. "The Sullivans will track Christine down before the month is over, and put this nonsense to bed. If Christine doesn't want to play nice, then neither will we." She drained the remainder of her julep in affirmation. "Is Amelia angry? About sending Oz into her head?"

"She says she isn't. On the surface, it may even be true. She's grateful to be alive, and understands she would not be had I not made the difficult decision. But the world she returned to is heartbreaking, and confusing for her. And that *is* my fault." Colleen played with a mint sprig peaking from her glass. "You know, Olivia came to visit me, before the world fell apart. Accused me of always putting my nose where it doesn't belong. She told me 'I hope, one day, Amelia sees you for who you really are.' I wanted to slap the words from her mouth, Evie. But when I look at the ruins of our family, I can't help but wonder... is she right?"

"I can't stomach another morality debate, Leena." Evangeline reclined in her wicker rocker, flapping the fan faster.

"Amelia is alive, because of you. And even if the dreamwalking propaganda is all true, Amelia is quite possibly the strongest person in this family. You trained her to protect her mind, and her heart, so she could be resistant to things which might otherwise hurt her. She's going to be fine. Truly."

"Both our girls will be," Colleen concluded wisely. *Then why can I not shake the feeling more disaster lurks under the surface?*

"I don't know if I should stay in New Orleans or return home with Johannes," Evangeline said. "I may be fooling myself into thinking Kat needs me, but I hold out hope she'll let me near her. At least to heal her so she can walk again!"

"Katja remaining in that wheelchair is her way of punishing herself," Colleen replied knowingly. "When she's ready, she will come to one of us. And you should return home. You know I'll look after her, and Markus, of course. I'll keep you apprised of any changes."

Evangeline nodded, standing. In the humidity, her unruly hair resembled a wild animal after an afternoon on the plains. "I may. I'll sleep on it." She stretched, then looked at her sister while re-buttoning her top. "Have you considered it may be time to share the prophecy with Amelia?"

Colleen drew back. "You know the dangers. If Elizabeth could've confirmed who the male was... but he was only a child."

Evangeline made a disapproving sound. "You and I *both* know the young boy in the prophecy was Jacob. Elizabeth was afraid to confirm it because we spent years making her second-guess every detail, as we forced her to dissect it, piece by piece. Amelia's thirtieth birthday is coming soon, and that is the age Elizabeth's divination comes to realization, is it not?"

Colleen nodded. "It is. But if Jacob is the man in the vision, then Amelia will find her way to him with or without my intervention. That *is* how prophecies work, you know. And those are the rules."

"You and rules have such a dysfunctional marriage," Evangeline pestered. "Did you ever think, maybe, you play a role in helping them fulfill their destiny?" When Colleen didn't reply, she waved her hand, apparently realizing to debate with her older sister was an exercise in futility. "Prophecy aside, if you want to help Amelia, don't force a discussion on her unarmed. Perhaps you can appeal to her by learning more about dreamwalking, so you can help her deal with the residual effects."

Colleen listened, thoughtfully. "I've already exhausted my own reference materials."

"All but one," her sister replied, with a wicked grin. "Much as it pains you, you should go see Jasper."

"Pfft, that old sass would love for me to come begging for help," Colleen retorted, as they both erupted into peals of rare and much-needed laughter.

Evangeline laid a kiss on her forehead and said, "We can commiserate on the injustice afterward."

LATER, AS COLLEEN PREPARED HER WEEKLY CORRESPONDENCE, SHE received her second visitor that day, this one unexpected.

"Markus, what a lovely surprise!" she exclaimed, opening her arms to receive him.

"Have you talked to Uncle Connor?" Markus asked, returning the embrace.

Colleen frowned. "Why no, not in a week or so. Is everything okay?"

Markus paced the marble foyer, pursing his lips. "Tristan is a mess. There are nights he doesn't even bother coming home anymore. I'm trying to help him. Sometimes I catch up, and I can hide behind an illusion and watch over him. Other times, I feel like I'm several steps behind."

What could she even say? The list of problems to tackle was daunting, and it was no shock Tristan was acting out his grief through unhealthy behaviors. "This is a trying time for all of us—"

"I'm not here about Tristan, though," he interrupted, then flashed a sheepish smile in apology. "I'm here about Jacob."

"Jacob?"

"He found Tristan the other night and brought him home—"

"Oh, bless him!"

"—from a local underground fight club," Markus finished. The smile of relief died on her face.

"A fight club? Oh, Tristan..." Things were worse than she thought.

"He didn't get a chance to fight," Markus assured her. "And even if he had, it would've lasted all of ten seconds. But the problem isn't Tristan. It's Jacob. You get what I mean?"

Understanding dawned on Colleen as she realized what Markus was trying to tell her. "I see. But how do you know about his past?"

"Tristan told me. He read Jacob's mind long ago, before Amelia trained him how to protect his thoughts. Before they were dating. Tristan was looking out for her, you know, he wasn't trying to be rude."

"No, I'm sure he wasn't," Colleen replied, distantly. She, of course, knew the history from Jacob's own mouth. She'd sat across from him, all those years ago, and listened to him relay the tale of his fighting years. Amelia had proposed marriage, on a whim and Jacob had wanted to confess all his sins, in order to start with the slate clean and be a good husband to her.

As his love for Amelia grew, the hunger in his eyes died to a healthier glow. But if what Markus said was true... "Are you sure? Maybe he was looking after Tristan."

Markus laughed. "I'm sure. Tristan said Jacob was as shocked to see him, as he was to see Jacob." He leaned against the ceiling-to-floor grandfather clock, watching her. "There's a fight tonight, at the same club. My guess is he'll be there. And if he is, we need to stop him."

Colleen nodded, processing, considering what this all meant. "They'll never let me in a place like that." She couldn't resist chuckling at her pressed Armani suit and Louboutin heels.

Her nephew smirked. "I can make you look like whoever you wanna be," he reminded her. "Hell, if you wanna go in there and throw down, Aunt C, we can make that happen, too."

"Heavens no!" she declared, her hand rising to her throat in shock. "Showing up in an illusionment will be quite enough, thank you."

He shrugged, but a smile played at the corner of his mouth. "Your loss."

Evangeline's words from earlier had stayed with her. *Did you ever think, maybe, you play a role in helping them fulfill the vision?*

The trouble was discerning what involvement would aid the hand of fate, and what would impede it.

As she walked her nephew to the door, a thought struck her. "Markus, I know you love Amelia. But why are you taking up Jacob's cause?"

Markus paused in the doorway, arms crossed over his chest. "Amelia and I have work to do." The mysterious tone was clearly intentional, but she decided to play along.

"What's the nature of your work together?"

"It's between us, for now. But she's not going to be ready until we can fix what's broken."

Colleen nodded, understanding.

8

JACOB

Jacob decided unpacking the boxes immediately, and quickly, would be easier than waiting and watching them sit piled in a corner, a cardboard shrine reminding him of a life no longer his.

There was a rock permanently lodged in his chest where his heart once resided. Heavy and unrelenting, it was a cold and awful thing. When Jacob's father put bullets in his wife and kids, the stone took form. It softened when he met Amelia, but now he understood it had always been there. Waiting.

Fifteen boxes sat in the corner, the sum total of all the material possessions he'd collected over the course of his adult life, or at least those years that mattered. Ashley offered to help him unpack, but Jacob didn't have the heart to tell him most of the contents would be thrown out with the morning's trash collection. Jacob's switch to survival could only be flipped by unfailing commitment.

As he sorted through his history, shallow breaths and

cold sweats made the ache in his fists, and the itch in his shoulders, return with a vengeance. *One more box, and then I can satisfy this hunger.*

The final one was heaviest of all, and he opened it to find mostly paperwork. Flipping quickly, he rifled through copies of research papers, sketches he'd made over the years, and important documentation, like his naturalization papers. Wedged into one of his notebooks was a green folder.

Only Amelia used green folders, so he knew its inclusion must be a mistake. Then, on the label tab, he saw one word in black marker: *Jacob.*

Though it had his name on it, Jacob understood this wasn't meant for his eyes. But curiosity overcame him, in light of the many unanswered questions surrounding the past months.

When he opened it, the few contents slipped out, falling into his lap.

He picked up two plane tickets to Dublin, printed with his and Amelia's names, dated three months prior. *Just after we broke up. Before she got sick.* There were other printouts related to whatever trip she'd planned to Ireland. Itineraries. Holy Trinity Cathedral and Killian Castle in Killianshire. Two names, written in Amelia's messy scrawl: Father O'Connor and Sister Agnes.

And finally, also in her handwriting: *Ask Jacob about the Quinlans?*

"What the devil?" Jacob whispered as he gazed down at what was likely the remnants of Amelia's desire to reconcile. Remnants that, somehow, stopped mattering entirely after three months alone with Oz Sullivan.

To hell with this. Jacob dropped the folder, grabbed his keys, and headed toward Algiers.

THE GAMEMAKER OFFERED NO PLEASANTRIES AS THEY DESCENDED the filthy staircase.

"I don't know what Vasily told you, but we don't play to technique the way your Russkie friends do. We don't care about rules. You wanna bite? Bite. Fancy yourself a kicker? Kick that motherfucker square in his motherfucking jaw, for all we care. But there are two, and only two, ways to end a fight."

"Dying and crying?" Jacob quipped, itching to get at it already as dust and sweat filled his nostrils.

The man stopped and eyed Jacob, top to bottom. "I imagine *you'll* be crying before the night's out." He laughed. "Two ways. First, a man can tap-out whenever he wants. No questions asked. He might not get asked to another fight, but we respect the tap-out here, because we don't respect much else. Second is if a fighter loses consciousness. When a man goes down, you stop. We square?"

"We are," Jacob agreed, lifting his tweed cap and hanging it on the crude hanger made of nails on a piece of plywood. "Are they wrapped?"

The man shook his head. "This is bare-knuckle, bare-foot fighting. No tape. No gloves. No padding. No brass. Nothing."

Jacob nodded. It was just as well. He preferred nothing to soften the pain. He didn't come here to play.

As they rounded a corner, the cries from the men grew louder, the cloying scents of blood and sweat, both fresh and stale, became almost putrid. It had been years since Jacob had last been in a makeshift arena like this, and the smells seemed foreign, yet somehow comforting, like returning home after a long absence.

The two men in the ring looked to be very nearly done, both covered head to toe in blood, fists quivering in the final throes of battle.

"Finish him, Getty!" one observer yelled, followed by a rousing cry of support from over half the room. *I guess they've all bet on him.*

Getty winked and then launched himself into a flying roundhouse kick that sent the room into a crazy uproar, as his opponent flew into the half-wall, slid to the ground, and then, slowly, tapped twice against the cement floor.

Getty proceeded as if being offered a championship belt by Don King himself, bloody arms raised in the air, stirring applause. This was not the fighting Jacob was used to. These men were here for the blood sport, and the thrill of measuring whose proverbial dick was bigger. They didn't understand the intrinsic connection between a man and his fist. The connection between a man's fist and the rock in his chest.

I want him. This Getty fellow. He's mine.

"Him," Jacob said to the bouncer, pointing at Getty. "How do I get in the ring with him?"

The man laughed. "Hey, Getty. This runt wants a go."

Getty's smile widened, as he finished his championship parade, and his eyes fell on Jacob. "This little Uptown shit-face? Really, George?"

George shrugged. "Up to you."

Getty smiled once more, revealing a mouth full of red teeth. “Rock and roll.”

Jacob ignored the cockiness radiating off the man, and equally drowned out the cajoling and laughter from the room as they joined in predicting what was, in their estimation, bound to be a complete walkover.

The calm started behind his eyes, then radiating down, down, into his shoulders, sending ripples of tranquility through his arms, and into his fingertips.

He let Getty throw the first punch. That initial shock to the system was a ritual Jacob used to employ to get himself worked up.

Jacob both felt and heard the crack as his nose broke. *Damn. Earlier than I’d hoped.* But adrenaline and blood rushed to his face, to his chest, to his hands, to his mind, as his feet started to dance on their own accord, his fists tightening to a close.

“Not gonna tap-out?” Getty mocked, matching his footwork, as he taunted Jacob with several feint jabs.

“You’ll know when the fight’s over,” Jacob promised, and then sent his right fist square into Getty’s grinning jaw, followed by an undercut left that threw the man stumbling back several feet, as his peers caught him.

When Getty came back up, he was no longer smiling. “Fuck the rules. You’ll have to get on your knees and beg if you want mercy.”

It was Jacob’s turn to smile. “I’ll let ye stick to playing on yer knees,” he said, and didn’t hesitate, throwing several stiff jabs, finished by a hard straight left, while Getty worked up a clever response.

Getty stumbled to his knees, wavering as he brought

back a hand containing one bloody tooth. "You son of a whore!"

No rules, Jacob thought, as he swung his leg in a powerful arc, foot connecting with Getty's face, while the man still nursed his prior wounds. And then again. And again. One connection after another, first a kick to the jaw, and then Jacob was on *his* knees, also, delivering rhythmic overhand strikes, not realizing until strong arms pulled him away that Getty had tapped out long ago, and now lay, motionless, on the cement.

Jacob's heightened pulse nearly came to a crashing halt, until he saw Getty move, slithering to the left to find a dignified place to pull himself up.

"Did you not hear me when I told you the rules?" George shook his head. "First and only warning."

Jacob nodded, as he caught snippets of the stunned words around him. Some couldn't believe he had laid flat a man they thought to be the best fighter among them. Others wanted their own go at the arrogant newcomer.

Let them all have a go tonight. I'll take the whole lot of 'em, if it makes the rest of this pain go away.

Several fighters were rushing George, asking to go next against the "Uptown shitface" who'd humiliated Getty.

Two more he fought. The first was quick and wiry, an inside fighter, but his lack of experience betrayed him early. He clearly telegraphed each of his moves, leading with his chin, giving Jacob the immediate advantage. The second was a burly man who Jacob supposed spent his days working on appliances but not much else. Clearly a catchweight match, but Jacob discounted the size difference. It was nothing to dance around and wear him out, the way his father taught him. The way he'd flattened Speck nearly two decades before.

After, George told him more wanted a go. "I'm fine to tell 'em no. Three is more than most do in an evening."

Jacob shook his head, spitting a mouthful of blood into the bucket beside him. "Aye, but I'm no' most. Keep 'em comin'."

The fourth fighter was as large as the last man, but fit as a butcher's dog. Jacob grinned, knowing he could never match the man fist-for-fist, but he would wear him out eventually.

As the first punch connected with Jacob's jaw, images of the expired plane tickets played across the space of his thoughts. *Father O'Connor* and *Sister Agnes*, written in Amelia's charmingly terrible script. *She'd done it all, for me. Tracked down the only other people in the whole world who mattered to me.* He pictured himself introducing Amelia to Sister Agnes, connecting those two worlds. Rescuing the fair maiden from his childhood imagination, whom he'd always, deep down, believed was really Amelia. Wearing his love for her on his sleeve, proudly, for the world to know.

A powerhouse uppercut knocked him off his guard. He scrambled to regain his footwork.

And then stopped.

He no longer wanted to win.

He no longer wanted to fight.

He was done.

He only wanted the cold ache in his chest to end.

Jacob planted his feet and spread his arms wide, baring his bloody chest free of defense. The man rushed him, smashing him into the wall so roughly it pushed the breath out of him. Then he stood as one brutal punch after another connected with his face, and torso, shoulder. He laughed as the blood ran out of his mouth, down his lips trickling to his chest. Finally, the rabbit punch to the back of his neck—a highly illegal move if this was a regulation match—drew stars in his vision.

"He's going to kill you!" someone shouted. "Tap out already!" said another.

Even George, who Jacob caught from his peripheral, wore an expression of deep concern.

This was the last thing he saw before everything went black.

Tiny bright orbs floated above Jacob.

"Jacob, darling, you're awake!" cried the ugliest man Jacob had ever seen.

"We need to get you out of here," muttered another man he didn't recognize. This one stood up and slipped a large bill to George, who nodded, then flashed a short smile at Jacob. It was the patronizing expression one offered a man who didn't have long to live.

"Who the bloody hell are you?" Jacob asked, too weak to fight the second man who now struggled to lift him.

"Shh," the first man hushed him. "Wait until we get to the car."

He lost consciousness again, regaining it when his head bounced against leather. He looked up to see Amelia's mother staring down at him, and he jumped. "Jesus, Colleen, ye nearly sent my heart crossways!"

"Oh look, his Irish came back," Markus chimed in, slipping into the driver's seat. "Can you lie still long enough for us to get you somewhere safe?"

Jacob tried to respond, but all he could see was the overwhelmingly solemn face of Colleen watching him with genuine love, and concern, as his vision first blurred and then the world slipped away once again.

9
TRISTAN

For the past week, Tristan had started the day with a killer headache and bruises he couldn't recall earning. His location had been different each day. A park bench, curled up next to a homeless man's bucket drums, underneath an empty stall at the French Market. But each temporary bed had one thing in common: they were not home.

Home, though, was a matter of perspective now. Tristan no longer considered the house he'd grown up in to be his home. He had always been alone, in all the ways that mattered, and now he was also completely on his own.

To his surprise, his father hadn't forgotten their last discussion. For days, Connor left messages on Tristan's phone, pleading with him to come home, to accept his help. Apparently, he had Markus tasked with the same goals. Tristan was beginning to believe perhaps his father *had* woken up, finally, when the calls stopped. Several days had passed since the last attempt. *He's a Sullivan lawyer, with access to the Deschanel funds. If he wanted to find me, it wouldn't be hard. I haven't left the city, and I haven't exactly been quiet in my comings and goings.*

Despite access to a limitless trust fund, his dad putting a stop on the credit card only momentarily pausing the fun, four bars now had permanently excommunicated Tristan. This included the one where he'd thrown up on Markus, who he now understood was the old man, as he was also the young woman in another bar, and the businessman in the next. *Oh well. A bar is a bar. Liquor is liquor. This is New Orleans, the Big Easy. I could drink in a new bar every day for the next three years and never the same one twice.*

It was long past bedtime for all the working-class stiffs, so the bar he currently occupied was nearly empty. Only the few diehards, like Tristan, remained. The nondescript blonde bartender poured him another whiskey, and he swilled it down, holding the shot glass out for a refill. He thought that was eleven shots, but he'd lost count around eight.

Tristan's phone buzzed. Markus' name lit up the screen. He'd only had one conversation with Markus since waking in the bed of that first strange woman. A small part of Tristan, the part still in control, was determined to never end up in an unfamiliar bed again. There existed the terrifying potential of what could result in such a foolish act; what *had* resulted from carelessness with Emily. No, as long as the Curse existed, there would be no more accidents. And therefore, no sex, which didn't bother him nearly as much as it should have.

He punched the ignore button, and then a text popped up: *Jacob is in trouble. Thought you should know.*

Tristan placed the phone facedown on the bar, and tipped his chin at the bartender. "Why don't you just load me up with several rounds, so I don't have to keep bugging you?"

A WARM BREEZE RUSHED OVER TRISTAN'S FACE, COAXING HIM OUT of his stupor. The smell of old beer and urine wafted up through his nostrils as his head registered the unpleasant fact it was lying on pavement. Squinting, he looked up into the moonlight. There were three bright white orbs beaming down on him. He closed one eye, and saw four. Then three again.

He checked his phone to see what time it was, but couldn't focus on the moving screen. Slipping his hands underneath him, he slowly pushed to a sitting position, gripping the nearest streetlamp to keep from tumbling back over. After several unsuccessful attempts to pull himself up, he rolled on to his stomach and pushed himself upright that way. Finally standing, he looked down and noticed his shoes were missing.

"Fuck," he whispered, but forgot his annoyance, already stumbling down the quiet alley, searching for any signs that would indicate his location. Everything he focused on washed in front of him in a blur of colors. His feet would connect with something foreign and he'd mindlessly kick it to the side. At some point he realized his left sock was bloody, the sodden fabric squishing audibly between his toes, but his brain wasn't registering pain.

When it seemed as if he had been hobbling down the alley for hours, he at last saw a car pass in front of him and knew he was coming to an intersection where he might be able to get his bearings.

"Charrrturrrrrrs," he sounded out as his eyes spotted a sign. Chartres Street. What was significant about this? Something... but what?

Ahh, yes! His car! Tristan had parked his car in the parking spot assigned to his cousin, Ana. She owned an apartment there, but was overseas, her own vehicle parked at Uncle Augustus' place in the Garden District. Tristan knew the car would be safe there; security patrolled the gated apartments. They only hassled him momentarily, until they realized who he was. *One of the few times I've been excited about being a Deschanel.*

With newfound enthusiasm, Tristan jogged haphazardly down the street, zigging and zagging, bumping into posts and poles along the way. He needed to drive. More than that, he needed to *leave*. To get out of town. Drive until he was far enough away from New Orleans that no one would raise an eyebrow at the names Sullivan or Deschanel.

A beacon of excitement burst through. This was the answer all along: To leave! To leave everyone, and everything. Why had he not realized it before? The answer had been in front of him, and so simple, all along.

He couldn't get to the car fast enough. His freedom, his very survival, depended on it. Now that the idea was in his head, he couldn't bear to wait a moment longer.

At last he spotted the tall, wrought iron gates of the community. Hobbling over, he chaotically punched in Ana's code and slipped inside, stumbling over a bush as he trip-jogged to his car. He dropped the keys several times before finally making connection, unlocking the car and awkwardly climbing inside. The BMW roared to life.

He threw the car into reverse, immediately jolting sharply as his vehicle connected with another behind him. The wail of the offended car's alarm pierced through his skull, and he panicked, pushing forward into a different car. He repeated this real life game of ping-pong several times before finally maneuvering the now battered vehicle through the gates, and tearing out into Chartres Street, narrowly missing another parked car.

"*Vivra sa vie*!" Tristan cried as he wove in and out of traffic, causing cars to veer right and left to avoid him. Tristan didn't notice any of it. He only felt the rush of adrenaline and the wind coursing past his face, through the open windows.

Get away... get away... get away from it all. Escape, forever, goodbye assholes!

These were Tristan's last thoughts before his car smashed headfirst into brick.

10

COLLEEN

"You remember the last time I healed you?" Colleen asked Jacob, as she tenderly nestled the ice pack above his brow.

He nodded his puffy head almost imperceptibly. One of his eyes had swollen shut, his left cheekbone cracked, nose pointed decidedly too far to the left. The blow to his cervical vertebrae was nearly enough to kill him, his adrenaline the only thing keeping him conscious. This was to say nothing of the evident damage to his rib cage, which should have protected his vital organs if he hadn't allowed someone to kick them in. *If we'd arrived much later... he meant to let them kill him.*

"Then you know this isn't immediate," she affirmed, placing both hands gently against the side of Jacob's face, as Markus paced nearby. "It could be days, perhaps weeks, for the worst of it to heal."

The broken man nodded once more. His breaths wheezed, and Colleen surmised he may have punctured a lung. She'd healed men worse off than Jacob—the motorcyclist who collided with a semi truck came to mind—but this was a man she considered family as much as anyone she shared blood with. She might need to call Evangeline to provide some supplemental healing, hopefully speeding the repair of his most serious injuries.

"I've called your sister. She's on her way," Noah declared, striding into the room and carefully kneeling before Jacob in one move. "What were you thinking, kid?"

Colleen smiled at her husband, who, though possessing no special abilities of his own, was somehow always in tune with her needs. Always had been, since the early days of their romance, in college in Scotland. "Thank you, darling."

Jacob muttered something incoherent in Noah's direction, who shook his head sadly. "*This* isn't the answer, son. But you already know that. Everyone knows you can't tell an Irishman nothin'." He glanced up at Colleen, who had already closed her eyes to begin her channeled focus. "Should I also call Luther? He's bad off, Leena."

Markus stopped pacing. "Call whoever you need to call. Hell, call all the healers. If Amelia sees him like this, she's going to flip the fuck out."

Colleen nodded at her husband, and he went to do as asked.

"Now shh," she admonished Markus, who resumed wearing out the floor. "I need complete silence."

Have you ever considered it may be time to share the prophecy with Amelia?

You know the dangers.

Glancing at Jacob, the only dangers she observed were the flashes of wild recklessness in his eyes, and the damage he'd willingly done to himself in order to forget a greater pain.

You and I both know the boy in the prophecy was Jacob.

Colleen hadn't forgotten the prophecy, but she *had* shoved it down, deep down, where it couldn't cause any havoc by inadvertently influencing her. She knew better than anyone that to interfere with a seer's vision, for the good or worse, was to invite tragedy. For this reason she avoided letting it build up her hopes when Amelia lay dying. It would have been so easy, so temptingly easy, to remind herself Amelia *couldn't* die, because she had a future to fulfill, likely with the man who now lay broken under Colleen's powerful hands.

Damn Elizabeth for providing so few details. How am I to know if saving this man is me playing god, or simply a part of fate's plan all along?

An hour later, four of Colleen's relatives had come and gone, each laying their hands on Jacob, one by one: Evangeline, Luther Fontenot, Leander Broussard, and Alton Guidry.

Jacob looked hardly better than he had before he'd been touched by healers, but Colleen knew the magic was doing its work. By morning, he wouldn't be nearly so terrifying to look at. By tomorrow afternoon, he may even be able to see out of both eyes.

"Thank you," Jacob winced, adjusting his position on the couch. "I wasn't askin' anyone to bail me out of my bad choices, but I appreciate it."

Colleen laid her hand gently over his, offering a loving pat. "You're a member of this family, no matter what happened." *Perhaps, even, an instrument of its salvation.* "And you're a good man, Jacob Donnelly. None of us would ever leave you to flail alone."

"And we're square. For Tristan," Markus added.

"That wasn't a place for a kid like Tris," Jacob replied. "He would've gotten himself killed."

Markus smirked. "But it's fine for you to have a death wish."

Jacob didn't respond to the barb, and Colleen's heart ached for the young man's deep-running shame. She couldn't comprehend the desperation, but she needed to.

"Jacob, what could have possibly put you in such a state, to drive you back to that?" Colleen pressed. It was not simply the loss of Amelia. Jacob's hotheadedness ran on impulse. There was a recent trigger, and she would ferret it out.

"I wanted to leave New Orleans," he hedged. She'd never known Jacob to lie, but it was evident he was avoiding a direct answer. "E'ery morning, I wake up, and I think, *This is the day. I'll do it today.* And somethin' keeps me from doing it, each time."

"What keeps you?" Colleen asked. She caught the eye-roll Markus tossed her way. *So what if the answer is obvious? He needs to hear himself say it.*

"We both know," Jacob answered. "It isn't tha' I think I can win her back. Amelia is the most stubborn woman I know, when she sets her mind to somethin'. But somethin' hasn't been sittin' right with me since she woke up." He grimaced as a wave of pain ripped through him. The healing wasn't all sunshine, especially when one was as damaged as

Jacob. "It's not jealousy, if tha's what ye think. She's a right to do as she pleases."

"Fascinating," Markus mused. "Your accent. One night of fighting and you've returned home to the motherland."

Colleen shot him a look. "I don't think that. And there's nothing to be jealous of," she mollified, transferring the ice pack to the left side of his face.

"No? I think there is, though I trust Amelia when she tells me she's not involved with Oz," Jacob replied, making an apparent effort to neutralize his unintentional brogue.

"Haven't you told him?" Markus asked Colleen, stopping to come closer. "You haven't. And why not? He deserves to know."

Shame had kept her from telling Jacob what she knew about dreamwalking. But before she could open her mouth to rectify the situation, Markus continued.

"Amelia is confused. *Really* confused. The dreamwalking saved her, probably—who really knows?—but it also messed her up. She and Oz are now bound to each other, in some sick and bizarre co-dependent shit-storm, and it might not be reversible. And somehow Oz convinced her that to survive she had to let *you* go."

"Markus, this probably wasn't the best time. He's in no state of mind—"

Jacob put a mangled hand up. "No, it's good you told me. I was right to be confused about her behavior. And it explains what I found tonight."

Colleen and Markus perked up. "What did you find?" they asked in unison.

Jacob drew in a deep breath, then cried out in pain as the air filled his damaged lungs. "Plane tickets. Plans to visit

Ireland. All arranged after we broke up, but before she got sick. I don't know precisely what she was planning, but what I saw was clearly not the work of someone who's saying goodbye. Then she did."

Colleen didn't know exactly what her daughter had been planning, but she had a pretty good idea.

I'm going to make things right, Mom. He's going to be so surprised. I promise I'll tell you as soon as I've told him, but I know it will make you happy, too.

What would make me happiest is to see you wed to the man you're meant for, Mia. Do you remember the drawings you made as a girl? Of the castle, and the young maiden?

No...

Well, you will, soon enough. And if you do not, I shall tell you, because there was foretelling in them. But it can wait, darling. Go, make your plans and we will talk later.

Colleen could hear her daughter's beaming smile from the other end as she said, *I can't say anything else, but you'll be pleased.*

"Jacob, I..." *I'm sorry. This is my fault. For panicking, and not better exploring the options. For not learning more about dreamwalking upfront, so I could prepare Oz, and tell him to advise Amelia to shield her mind.* "I don't have an answer right now, but we *will* address the situation. For now, I need you to rest so the healing can do its work."

Jacob put up no argument. His puffy eyes started to droop, and his voice was muddy with exhaustion.

Colleen nodded at Markus, who stood perched against the marble mantle, watching Jacob with sad concern.

"I've got him," he assured her, and she left to call Amelia.

What else had Elizabeth said? That Amelia and her beau

would endure a great trial before finding their way to one another.

It was time to tell her about Elizabeth's premonitions, and the link to Amelia's own visions as a girl. She'd hoped her daughter would remember them on her own, but circumstances forced her hand.

Amelia deserved to know. It was her life, her future. Her fate.

"Aunt C." Colleen's niece Anne appeared at the top of the stairs, with a troubled expression. "I couldn't help but overhear some of what was going on. Can we talk?"

"Of course, dear. What's on your mind?"

"In private?" Anne beseeched.

After setting the phone in its cradle, Colleen ascended the long, wide staircase and followed her niece into the younger woman's suite. Anne had lived with Colleen for several years. An untrained arborkinetic, and illegitimate issue of Colleen's deceased older brother, Charles, Anne had emerged seeking family, and answers. Colleen eagerly gave her both, though the transition hadn't been easy.

"Is Jacob going to be okay?" Anne inquired, as Colleen closed the door behind them.

"He should make a full recovery in about a week," Colleen answered, though his skin and bones were only half the equation. "What's going on, Anne?"

Anne's expression had metamorphosed from concerned to troubled on the walk to her room. She wrung her hands over her stomach, looking down. "Something isn't sitting right with me. I hadn't said anything before, because I worried I might be overreacting. But now I'm not so sure."

"Go on," Colleen urged, guiding her toward the bed, to sit.

"Adrienne was acting really strange before she died. I know now she was keeping her illness a secret, but it was more than that. She even invited me over for some 'sister time,' out of the blue, and then started hinting about all these bad things she'd done. Things Oz didn't know about."

Adrienne soliciting her sister for company *was* odd, but Colleen would never say it for fear of hurting Anne, especially on so fresh a loss. "It's normal for people to feel regret when they know their death is imminent," she assured her niece. "It's an emotionally overwhelming time for most, full of doubt, and questioning. Many evaluate their choices in life, and wonder how they could have done things differently."

Anne shook her head. "It was more than that. She seemed like she was ready to *confess* something, and had we not been interrupted, well, I think she might have told me."

Colleen tucked a lock of hair behind her niece's ear. "I wouldn't let it trouble you, dear. Each of us has things we'd prefer to take back."

But Anne could not be assuaged. "And then... I went to *Ophélie* today, to check on how things were coming along. Well, mostly to check on my brother, and Nicolas told me something I haven't been able to get out of my head."

"What did he say?"

Anne continued, tentatively. "You know he was with Adrienne in her final moments." Colleen nodded. "He told me Ade said some really strange things before she died. He thought it was gibberish, but after my last conversation with her... and after what I overheard tonight... well, I'm not so sure, Auntie."

Colleen sensed her niece was feeling rebuffed by her gentle downplaying earlier, so she straightened her posture, and folded her hands in her lap, attentive. "You have good senses, Anne. If it's bothering you, then it matters."

"Well, apparently Adrienne told him she wanted Oz and Amelia to get together after she died. And when Nic laughed it off and said Amelia was just as ill as Adrienne was, Adrienne quite seriously told him Amelia was going to wake up soon. Not minutes later, Amelia did."

Colleen hadn't known what to expect from Anne, but this was not it. "Why didn't Nicolas say something sooner?"

"He thought she was rambling," Anne explained. "He never guessed there might be some substance in the words. He doesn't have the context we do."

"You were right to tell me this," Colleen responded, mulling over all the confusing pieces of this puzzle. She didn't know how any of them fit. Not yet.

Anne looked relieved. More than that, unburdened. "Thank you. Let me know if I can help."

"I will, darling."

Much as it pained her, Colleen accepted it was time to speak with Jasper.

11

AMELIA

A slight breeze whipped across the plain, carrying the sounds and scents of merriment from the gathering in the valley below. Cerridwen glanced up at the Norman tower, which shone like a recently polished copper pot against the full moon's light.

Inside, Cianán awaited her. Of course, in this lifetime he was not Cianán, but Doran, just as she was Moira, not Cerridwen. Thirty lifetimes they had lived and loved, and her heart never grew tired, or weary, of his steadfast loyalty and protection. But in each iteration, it became harder to find their way to one another. The memories of who they once were faded gradually with each rebirth. Eventually, they would forget altogether.

The goddess visited her dreams, assuring these fading memories were part of their fate. That one day, many, many, many years from now, they would find one another, with no memory at all. Then, after overcoming terrible odds, they would fulfill their fate.

Cerridwen trusted her goddess and accepted the prophecy.

She sang along with the Quinlans when they remembered the sacred love of Cianán and Cerridwen, and of their destiny to reunite what had been laid asunder.

But as her memory faded, fears took root in her heart. She knew the time was coming, soon, when she would be again born into this world, and this time she would not know her Cianán when she saw him. She would have to trust to her goddess, and the power of their enduring souls, to bring him to her.

With a heavy heart, Cerridwen climbed the stone steps, for the final time in this lifespan, to once again die beside her soul's other half.

"Síoraíocht, a stór."

AMELIA'S DREAM STAYED WITH HER ALL DAY. THE FAMILIARITY OF Cianán and Cerridwen. The feeling they were both an intrinsic part of her. Who they were, or what relevance they held, remained beyond her grasp.

A tenuous air still existed between Amelia and her mother, but in her time of need, she was the first person Amelia turned to. At minimum, her mother could put her mind at ease.

And if there *was* something to these visions, no one was better equipped to guide her.

AMELIA PUSHED OPEN THE HEAVY DOOR OF THE GARDENS TO FACE A startled Aria.

"Hi, Aria," Amelia greeted, offering a quick embrace. "I see my mother's town car is gone. Is she not here?"

The normally unruffled Aria struggled for words,

releasing several choked sounds before pointing first toward the sitting room, then shaking her head furiously, and instead gesturing up the stairs.

With a curious look, Amelia moved past her, into the sitting room. As soon as she entered, her eyes locked onto a panicked look from Markus that matched Aria's. She followed his gaze to the couch, where a battered Jacob grimaced as he struggled with a glass of water.

"Donnelly!" Amelia cried, all distance, words, and decisions made between them lost in her alarm at seeing him in such a state. She collapsed on her knees, hands dancing before his face, wanting to touch him, fearful of hurting him further. "What *happened* to you?"

Markus' steady footfalls sounded on the soft wood as he left the room.

Jacob set the glass down, and reached forward with his right hand, squeezing hers as it hovered in the air. "*Blanca,* it's nothing," he insisted, the way he always had, no matter how much trouble he was in.

"We both know that's a lie," she whispered, as her understanding of the situation slowly formed into a clear picture. Both hands, wrapped and swollen to triple their intended size, the shame and exhilaration fighting within him.

"Your mom is an insistent lady," Jacob grinned, a grotesque gesture accentuated by a cracked jaw and swollen lips. His smile faded. "She called in the cavalry. I feel terrible about causing such a ruckus."

Amelia shook her head, as she tasted the first of her own salty tears. "I'm so glad she did," she contended. "What were you *thinking*?"

Despite his condition, she didn't miss the familiar sparkle in his eye, or the light sigh behind his words. "That it's time for me to leave New Orleans."

Amelia opened her mouth to protest, but to do so would be selfish. It was plain they couldn't go on the way they had been. "Did you win?"

Jacob's bruised face cracked into another haphazard grin. "Aye. All but the last one."

Amelia returned the smile, her thoughts back on the early days of their friendship, when he still ventured out to fight clubs on the weekends. He'd stumble to her dorm room, bloody but alive with pride. She'd tenderly dress his wounds, listening to his stories of the evening. As they grew closer, she could always feel, with her sixth sense, when he was off engaged in his blood sport. Over time, his pride and excitement evolved to shame, as his love for her put down roots.

"I should've sensed this," she lamented, realizing he still held tight to her hand. Reluctantly, she released him. "I don't even know who I am anymore."

The smile he gave her this time lit up his whole face, and for a moment she could see past the breaks and bruises. "I do. You're the same feisty empath who can't stand to lose a bet, and who has a less than stellar reputation in the kitchen."

His teasing caught her off guard, producing an unexpected laugh. He laughed with her. "Maybe some things don't change," she admitted, sniffling.

"You gave me the best ten years of my life, Amelia. Everything has a season, I guess." The words were more for himself than her. “But there is one thing I’d like to know. I found—”

Her phone rang, putting a halt on the moment. She flashed Jacob an apologetic look, and answered. As she listened to the voice on the other end, her face reelecting her growing horror, Jacob’s expression turned from curiosity to concern.

“What is it?” he asked, reaching for her hand again.

Instinctual. This new life feels surreal to both of us.

“It’s Tristan. He’s had an accident.” Her hands shook as she failed to slip her phone back in her purse. Jacob reached forward, steadying her. “I have to go.”

“I’m coming with,” he asserted, and was hobbling out the door before she could argue.

TRISTAN HAD BEEN FLOATING IN AND OUT OF CONSCIOUSNESS SINCE the night before. Amelia, Jacob, and Markus, sat patiently waiting for him to fully awaken. Amelia noted, with grateful relief, that Jacob’s wounds had healed tremendously overnight. Indulging herself, she held his hand lightly in hers, an anchor.

“Tristan’s been in an accident,” her cousin Olivia had said the night before on the phone, with a touch of exasperation. Olivia was a seer, but loathed her ability, just as she loathed most of her family. “I saw it. You should probably find him since that Sullivan of a father he has is talking to walls and God knows what else.”

Amelia was grateful Olivia had taken the time to call. Her cousin had been wrapped up in her own grief after losing her brother, Alain, to suicide. Olivia spent her days at Katja's bedside, helping her care for the twins.

Watching Tristan now, hooked up to all the monitors, Amelia was glad she'd had the foresight to call her mother on the way over. He was in critical condition when they brought him in: broken bones, punctured lung, brain edema, internal bleeding. When Colleen pulled the chart from the ER doctor's hand, he told her sadly that the young man might not survive the night. Dr. Colleen Deschanel insisted on her own assessment, and so slipped alone into his room.

Amelia had never seen a wound her mother couldn't assuage; no physical illness she couldn't soothe. In fact, other than a troubled mind, the only malady her mother was unable to cure was death itself. A few hours later, and that might have been the challenge facing her, but Olivia's call had saved Tristan's life.

"Amwoah," Tristan whispered. The oxygen mask muffled his voice. *Amelia,* she felt him say. His mind was clear.

"I'm here," she said soothingly, wrapping both of her hands around his free one. "Just rest."

Tristan shook his head back and forth, his frantic breaths fogging up the translucent cup over his mouth. Amelia lifted the breathing mask, and he coughed, wheezing in a deep breath.

"I'm dead," he whispered hoarsely. "Right?"

Amelia chuckled softly. "You're far from dead. But you are in a lot of trouble."

His eyes moved around searchingly. Finding no coherent thought, he released a yawning sigh. "I don't remember much."

"Alcohol is funny like that," she said, and moved to put the cup back over his mouth. He shook his head again.

"You really need to rest," Amelia insisted.

"I need to get out of here," Tristan replied, once again looking around the room in a fresh panic. *He wants an escape. He wants to be far away from me, from this hospital. Scared. Aching. Wants a drink. He's considering running.*

She took a deep breath. Her eyes met Jacob's momentarily, and he gave her his silent support, as always. Markus rose without a word, and moved to inconspicuously block the view from the hall. "The cops are outside waiting for you to wake up," she told her cousin. "As soon as you're well enough to leave, you'll be arrested and charged."

"Charged for *what*?" Tristan demanded, his voice gritty and stilted.

"For some reason, people don't like it when you ram your car into the side of their restaurant," Markus spoke up. "They like it even less when the damages are extensive enough to shut down their business for weeks."

"Ugh," Tristan moaned. "It's a little fuzzy."

"I think we should call your father," Amelia suggested. Her eyes passed from Tristan, to the window, and back. Markus' methodical pacing would only mask so much. She worried one of the officers might peer in and see Tristan was alert. "You ran into Cutler's, Tristan."

Tristan's eyes widened in alarm. Cutler's was one of the oldest and most respected establishments in New Orleans. It rivaled Arnaud's in price and class, and Brennan's for age and reputation. They were also known for being highly litigious, and for having sued several smaller competitive restaurants out of business. There was little doubt in

Amelia's mind they'd be coming after Tristan. The lingering cops outside amplified her fears.

"We can't call my dad," Tristan said, more alert now. When he moved to stand, Amelia shook her head quickly, and he slipped back under the covers. "We aren't really talking right now."

"Then call one of your Sullivan uncles. Call Colin, call someone," Amelia whispered furiously. "Now is *not* the time to get sanctimonious about how you don't like to take advantage of where you came from!"

"I'll call Augustus," Jacob stated. "He'll take care of it."

"I don't want anyone calling anyone!" Tristan screeched, and as the cops turned their heads, Amelia diverted a quick, intense focus their direction, attempting to push their attention elsewhere. She was not a full telempath—one who could project feelings on to others—but sometimes she could make it work in short bursts. To her great relief, the officers went back to their discussion. *For now.*

"You need to stop acting like a child, Tristan," she scolded. *He hates me right now. He's changed so much.* "Yes, your life is fucked up. But look around you: everyone's lost someone! You've really messed up this time, and if you don't get over yourself, you're going to go to jail, possibly for a very long time. So, suck it up and accept our help, or we're done."

Tristan smiled impishly. "You're not really mad at me. You're just trying to be the mom I never had, boo hoo."

"Let's go," Markus said, reaching for the door handle. "He doesn't want our help."

"He doesn't have a choice," Amelia insisted, nodding at Jacob to make the call, so they could get the nonsense with the police and Cutlers' sorted. "He's coming home with us, where we can look after him."

Jacob raised an eyebrow at the use of "us," but then smiled and shook his head, seeming to realize it was nothing more than an innocent slip. He planted a brief kiss against her cheek on the way out. "I'll go call now."

"Thank you," she whispered. A magic stirred between their gazes, and she almost, for a moment, stopped caring about her convictions. Her defense was as weak in that moment as it had ever been. "Wasn't there something you wanted to ask me? Before we came down here?" she added hopefully.

Don't go. I don't care if this love is selfish anymore, I only want you. Just you. Always you.

He flashed her a sad smile as he opened the door. "It's not important," he replied, and then was gone.

Amelia swallowed back the wave of emotion forming, and returned her attention to Tristan.

12
OZ

Ashley's expression when he opened the door was paralytic. "Amelia asked you not to come here." He wedged himself across the narrow opening, as if he expected Oz to make a break for it and spring past him. "She has enough to deal with."

"I'm here to see Tristan," Oz countered. "It's been a week since his accident. He's my cousin, too."

Ashley's eyes narrowed, studying Oz's face for signs of deception. Then his expression softened slightly and he said, "Tristan is resting. He has a big day ahead of him tomorrow. I can tell him you stopped by, and he'll call when he's awake if you want to visit."

Oz nodded. "How is he?"

Everything about the man looked world-worn, even his shoulders as they lifted in a shrug. "I have a feeling his problems are only beginning."

"I've already talked to my father."

"Thanks, but not necessary," Ashley acknowledged.

"Uncle Augustus was able to get an emergency arraignment earlier this week, and Tristan's sentence was lighter than he deserved. Yay for persuasion, I guess." He exhaled, leaning into the doorframe. "I'm surprised you don't already know all this. And you can call Uncle Connor and tell him to stop coming over here. Tristan doesn't want to see him right now."

"Connor is his father," Oz protested. "You're not helping Tristan by keeping his dad away."

Ashley's whole body seemed to sigh. "Oz, it's late. I'll tell Tristan to call you when he wakes tomorrow."

Amelia appeared then, in an old Tulane sweatshirt and yoga pants. Oz's heart seized in an irrepressible response to her presence. "It's okay, Ash," she said. "I'll talk to him."

"Mia–"

She planted a kiss on his cheek. "Really, I'm fine."

"Stubborn Deschanel women," he muttered, but his mouth turned up in a slight smile. "I'm going up to bed, but I'll check on Tristan one more time."

Amelia nodded. "I will as well, before I turn in."

"Be careful," Ashley added, before excusing himself.

"He really doesn't like me," Oz noted, as Amelia closed the door behind her, stepping on to the porch.

"Ashley is a natural protector," she explained. The glow of the gaslight caught the flush in her cheeks and the shimmer of her white tresses, stealing Oz's breath. "His family isn't here for him to look after, so I'm the next best thing."

Amelia's face came into full view under the porch lights. Red rimmed lids, highlighting her bloodshot eyes. A deep, exhausted flush painting her cheeks.

"Do you still have some of that Jameson I brought you from Dublin?" she ventured, sniffling.

THEY SETTLED ON OZ'S BACK PORCH, AMELIA EASING INTO THE OLD rocker Adrienne was once so fond of.

Despite asking after his whiskey, she declined a glass when Oz handed her one.

"I'm going to *Ophélie* tomorrow to talk to Nicolas. I know the Runeans aren't arriving for another month or so, but I don't think he has the first idea how to get the property in order," she said, slumping on the wicker chair, knees pulled tight to her chest.

"I agree he could use your help," Oz mused with a half-hearted chuckle. "But if you're thinking it will make you forget about everything... well, it won't."

Her large, sad eyes implored him as she gazed from where her head rested sideways atop her drawn knees. "You forget, I've been pushing away the bad stuff all my life. If there were an Emotional Olympics, I'd take home the gold medal."

Oz smiled. "I bow before your expertise on the matter," he teased, "but some losses are meant to be felt."

"You're in no position to talk," she reminded him. "But I don't disagree. I think some losses *should* be felt, and you're not going to start your grieving process as long as I'm a stone's throw away."

Oz considered this, recalling his grandfather's words. "I don't know if having you close makes things easier, or harder," he replied. "The last thing I want is to be the cause of your anguish."

"You aren't," she assured him. "But you're not the cure, either."

All around them, the night was alive with the trills of frogs, crickets; the lyrical song of cicadas. But neither Oz nor Amelia said another word, the silence swallowing their worries.

Eventually, he heard her breaths lighten, and, realizing she'd fallen asleep, he placed a small throw over the top of her. Grabbing a second for himself, he took the chair next to her, and was asleep in minutes.

13
COLLEEN

"Thanks for meeting me on a Sunday, Jasper," Colleen said, folding her hands over her lap. Outside the bay windows, a summer storm berated the Garden District, bouncing off banana leaves and magnolia blossoms. Inside Commander's Palace, the jazz band's agreeable tunes grew closer as they made their way from one patron's table to the next. "I read about the hurricane turning ceremony they had in Bayou Sauvage. Shouldn't have been a surprise to me that you'd be there."

Jasper grinned, re-settling his cup in the small saucer. "And once again, the city avoided major disaster. People forget, Katrina turned at the end. It was our infrastructure which did us in." He sipped his spicy orange tea, slowly shaking his head with pleasure. "As for meeting today, we both know my spiritual proclivities leave me free on Sundays, as compared to our peers."

Colleen returned the smile, taking a sip of her own peppermint tea. Even though she sometimes had reservations about her cousin, there was an earnest sincerity to his eccentricity. Most saw his business as ridiculous, but she had no doubt in her mind Jasper truly believed he conversed with voodoo queen Marie Laveau. "How are the children?"

"Estella is still in Paris pursuing her occult studies. I think she may one day take my place," he boasted proudly. "Leander is... well, you know Lee. He helps down at the Coffer when he's not in class, but getting him to do anything is like pushing a boulder uphill."

Colleen nodded in understanding. "Leander is a special boy. Always has been. We certainly appreciated his help with Jacob recently. And Harriett?"

At the mention of his youngest daughter, Jasper frowned. Harriett, now twenty-one, had not spoken a single word since her seventh birthday. She communicated through a series of very specific facial expressions and drawings, which were often prophetic in nature. Rumors speculated that Harriett's silence was born of cruelty by her older sister, Estella, or even her mother, Pandora. Perhaps a combination of both. But it was also well-known that Jasper had been led around by both women for years, and so his view on what really went on behind his walls was tainted by their influence.

"She's in Magnolia Rest," he replied, with reluctance. Colleen knew, even before he said it, that this had again been the influence of Pandora. "Pan is overwhelmed with the business, and can't care for her properly. I fought the move initially, but she's right. Harriett hasn't changed in fourteen years, and perhaps we're making her worse? That's what Pandora thinks." He shook his head.

Your wife is making her worse, Colleen didn't say. "I'm not familiar with the facility. Who funds it?"

Jasper lifted his hands. "Pan did all the research. Said it was the best in New Orleans. All of South Louisiana, even. The whole thing is rather upsetting, to be completely candid, Colleen. A family of healers and no one can cure my mute daughter." The waiter placed the turtle soup before Colleen, and a crawfish and succotash appetizer in front of Jasper. "But you're the one who called this meeting. What can I help with?"

"You spoke with my niece, Olivia, some time back, regarding Oz and the discovery of his dreamwalking," she broached. Jasper nodded. "She walked away with the impression that Amelia and Oz would be left reliant on each other forever in some twisted symbiosis. I take it you remember this discussion?"

Jasper dabbed his face with the cloth napkin. "Yes, I recall the conversation. I must confess, I was having some fun with her. After her and her mother's outbursts at the Collective convocation, I couldn't help myself."

Colleen's tensions eased. "Ahh. So you lied to her. Then it isn't true."

Jasper shook his head, quickly chewing his food in order to respond. "No, it's absolutely true. Without a doubt. I only mean I embellished a bit."

Colleen pushed her soup away, untouched. "How do you mean?"

Jasper continued to attack his appetizer with ravenous aplomb. "I may have understated the existing relationships of the dreamwalkers and their targets. Most were very close prior to ever sharing dreamwalking, so the bonds formed were not entirely unforeseen." He laid his fork across the plate. "Colleen, if I caused you any heartburn over this, you have my deepest apologies."

She waved away his regret. "I can't say I'd have acted differently. Olivia has a way of making anything difficult, though she means well." She mulled his words over, beginning to piece together the impact of her choice.

Her thoughts must have been plain on her face. "If you're here because you think your decision to send the Sullivan kid into Amelia's head is what pushed her from her beau, you can rest easy," Jasper assured her. "It's no fallacy that dreamwalking brings two people closer together—much closer, in many cases—but if no groundwork was there prior, it's unlikely to form the same kind of irreparable bond found in the stories I shared with Olivia."

"That *is* a relief," Colleen acknowledged, exhaling a long sigh. "But this behavior is entirely unlike Amelia. If not the dreamwalking, then what?"

Jasper offered enthusiastic appreciation to the waiter as a bouillabaisse was set before him. Colleen's shrimp entrée was likely to remain as untouched as her soup. "My, this looks marvelous!" he exclaimed. "I must say, I haven't made occasion to visit Commander's in some time, so you have my gratitude for pushing me toward an old favorite."

Colleen patiently waited for him to enjoy his meal. Finally he said, "Truthfully, this doesn't sound to me like a result of dreamwalking. Perhaps some residuals, but I wouldn't expect it to cause the fervent devotion I'm hearing about, not to mention the complete personality departure from both of them."

"I can't argue with that," Colleen agreed. "For Amelia to

abandon Jacob, something significant must have intervened in her thought process. And Oz has always been a fine man. I can't fathom how he can be more caught up in his adoration for Amelia than mourning the loss of his wife, especially after all he and Adrienne went through to even be together. But yet, I have no other answers."

"It looks and sounds an awful lot to me like the work of a skilled illusionist," Jasper speculated through a mouthful of shellfish. "Someone with the power of influence at the caliber of, say, Augustus."

Colleen scoffed at the suggestion. "Augustus has no reason to be involved in this. Besides, he loves his niece."

"*Like* Augustus," Jasper clarified. "There aren't many with his level of skill."

"What are you suggesting, exactly? That someone planted these ideas in my daughter and Oz?"

"Perchance."

"But that's preposterous! Why would anyone *do* such a thing?"

Jasper shrugged. "As to a motive, it would be irresponsible to guess without knowing more. I only know this reeks of illusion."

Colleen had trouble wrapping her mind around this possibility. Who would do this, and why?

Except... Nicolas' last conversation with Adrienne was not something to be ignored. There was something to his unease, she knew it. More, she *felt* it.

"Oh, and before it completely escapes my mind again, you should stop in and see my sister, Imogen," he added. "She's claimed to have a seer's vision involving Amelia, though what she described made little sense to me. Really, it may be utter nonsense. She's been under considerable duress since the heart attack."

Another seer's vision involving my daughter.

She considered the revelations of the conversation as she watched Jasper slurp his bouillabaisse.

14
TRISTAN

Tristan stood in the shower, letting the hot water wash over him. He was dreading the day ahead. Had been since his arraignment.

The judge had been unusually lenient. Tristan knew why. This didn't make the sentence any less depressing, or undesirable.

Instead of feeling grateful he'd been born into not one, but two families who could save his ass, he felt a sense of shame. Not that he *wanted* to serve hard time behind bars. He was well aware that community service at an assisted living facility was about as close to walking free as he could expect, under the circumstances. But there was a part of Tristan that acknowledged his need to be punished for all he'd done. Both sides of him were at odds, and neither wanted to be going to Magnolia Rest for the next ninety days.

He was, however, grateful to Amelia and Ashley for taking him in without judgment. Not that he'd had much of a choice. It was either move in with them, or go back to his father's house. The house arrest terms were clear: he had to have a steady home. The only time he could leave said steady house was when he was at Magnolia Rest, or traveling to and from. If he was caught veering from his schedule or route, he would be thrown in jail. No plea bargains. No deals. Just a year of jail time. *You'll follow this plan,* Uncle Augustus had said, after the sentence was handed down, *or I'll not lift another finger to help you, ever again.*

A green flashing light caught his eye, and he remembered the uncomfortably tight, unfashionable bracelet he had to wear around his ankle. That was swell, too.

Tristan switched off the shower.

MAGNOLIA REST WAS MARKETED AS AN ASSISTED LIVING FACILITY "with all the comforts of home," and a final retreat for the well-off when they could no longer care for themselves. It boasted fancy trim, and well-manicured landscaping. On the inside, wainscoting trailed for miles. Crown molding sung to the hearts of the wealthy.

In reality, it was no different than any other retirement home. The staff was mildly unpleasant, the food barely edible, the overall mood somber. All that mattered was that the men and women who delivered their parents, and invalid relatives, walked away with a light conscience. Their slogan was, "Your loved ones are our loved ones." Checkmark for warm fuzzies.

Mildred, the head nurse, showed Tristan around the facility. "And here is where we have arts and crafts time!"

she exclaimed with an excited wave of her wrinkled hand. Mildred looked like she was a few bad summers from being a resident herself.

Tristan peered through the tempered glass. Zombies, all of them, going through the mechanical motions of Connect Four and checkers. No smiles, laughs, or joking in this room. "I don't see any arts and crafts," he said, frowning.

"Oh, we do that twice a week, on Tuesdays and Thursdays, dear," she said with a cluck of the tongue and moved him forward. "And this," she continued, pointing toward the next room, "is our Reading Escape!"

Tristan was already thinking about escape himself. There was no reading going on there, except the old man in the corner enjoying the newspaper upside down. There was, however, potted palms and even a grand piano, sans pianist, among the tropical decor.

From there, Mildred showed Tristan where the break room was, and all the other unmemorable things she thought he should know. Finally, the tour came to an end, and Tristan voiced the question he'd had since his sentence came down.

"So, what, exactly, am I going to be doing here?"

Mildred cocked her head to the right and smiled thinly. "No one told you?"

Tristan shook his head.

She gave a short, muted laugh followed by a slight roll of the eyes. "You're in for a treat. Follow me."

They briskly returned way they'd come, passing the break room and convalescing patients slumped in hallways. They reached the Reading Escape room again, and she gestured through the large, Plexiglas window.

"Harriett," she announced, and he followed her gaze to the corner of the room where a young woman sat on a loveseat, alone, staring out the window.

Tristan was speechless. Harriett was quite young. His age, or younger, even. She had long, dark hair, and a face that was both plain and doll-like. Even sitting, he could tell she was tall and thin, with wispy, winnowing limbs. Her expression was serene, but there was an emptiness to it that left a sinking feeling in his stomach. There was something familiar about the young woman, but he couldn't place it.

"Why is she here?" he asked. "She's so young. I don't understand."

"Nursing homes aren't just for us seniors," she explained with her signature tongue cluck. "We take in people of all ages who can't take care of themselves. Harriett, though, is our youngest."

Tristan opened his mouth to press further, but Mildred went on, "She came to us a couple of weeks ago. Her parents are Jasper and Pandora Broussard, you know."

The Broussards were distant relatives of the Deschanels, descendants of Blanche. Jasper was a Magi Collective Council member, and had always been nice to Tristan. He and his wife, Pandora, were well-known around New Orleans for their ridiculous occult business in the Quarter, where they ran ghost tours, palm readings, and other nonsensical tourist traps for fans of the supernatural. They'd grown filthy rich off the backs of tourists and unsuspecting locals who still believed in the power of magic. *Well, I've seen magic, and what they do at the Soothsayer's Coffer doesn't qualify.*

Tristan recalled only two children, Leander and Estella.

He didn't remember a third, though now he understood why Harriett was familiar.

Mildred continued, "The poor dears have cared for this child her whole life, giving her the best home two parents could, but she hasn't spoken a single word since she was seven. They've taken her to doctor after doctor, and there's been no change in her condition for fourteen years. That is, until she attacked her mother with a kitchen knife." Mildred shook her head, as if her pity lay with the parents and not the child. Rules be damned, Tristan focused in on her thoughts. *Children are such a burden, and this child specifically is so ungrateful. Though, we could never say no to such a generous donation, and she's no trouble even if her condition is too ridiculous to be borne.*

Tristan narrowed his eyes, feeling an unexpected protectiveness toward the girl. A nursing home was no place for her.

"So, what, she gets to rot here for the rest of her life?" Tristan demanded.

Or until the money runs out, he heard Mildred think. His fists clenched in his pockets. "Well, we do have doctors tending to her, and perhaps they can make progress where others didn't. You know, Magnolia Rest *does* have access to some of the best medical facilities in the entire state of Louisiana, and..." She rambled on but Tristan tuned her out. He already had the measure of Mildred.

"So, what does this have to do with me?" Tristan interrupted, still watching Harriett. The young girl tilted her head to the left. Her eyes closed, but she tapped her feet lightly on the linoleum.

Mildred clucked again, suggesting it was intolerable that

Tristan couldn't decipher her vague meaning through storytelling. "Well, the Broussards, great citizens and parents that they are, have paid extra to ensure Harriett gets... individualized care. For now, we've been rotating the nurses to sit with her, but we were looking for someone who could fill this duty full time."

Tristan noted that, despite their supposed rotation, Harriett had been alone the entire time they were talking. "So, you want me to... what? Read to her? Talk to her?"

Mildred looked annoyed. *You could drop her off a bridge if you want, so long as her parents keep helping with the bills,* Tristan distinctly heard. "Why, whatever you want!" she intoned, sweetly. "Nurse Shelby tells me she loves playing chess."

"And then what happens to her after my ninety days are up?"

We'll find some other drunken imbecile just like you to start the rotation all over again, her caustic thoughts rang. He wanted to be as far from Mildred as possible. There was a blackness to her; a rotting from the inside out.

"Don't you worry," she insisted, clucking her tongue. Tristan thought he might hear that sound in his nightmares. "Miss Harriett will receive the best we have to offer."

Moments later, when Mildred was gone, Tristan slowly walked into the room. Harriett's eyes were open again, gazing out the window. Upon closer look, he saw tears sparkling in her eyes. *What's your story, Harriett?*

Tristan blocked out his own thoughts, trying to read hers. The staticky, jumbled mental ramblings of the other residents came through clearly, but Harriett's mind was decidedly silent. As he approached her, he focused on blocking everything out but Harriett. The closer he got, the quieter the sounds became. Eventually, everything else was no more than a dull roar, like the deep lull of ocean currents from afar. But nothing from Harriett.

“Hi,” Tristan greeted, shyly, taking the seat across from her. She looked at Tristan with her bright blue eyes and smiled. She reached out quickly and patted his hand twice with hers, then sunk back into her chair.

Moments later, she seemed to forget he was there and went back to her window gazing.

15
JACOB

Jacob's healing progressed at a nice pace, thanks to the Deschanels. He'd thought of them as his own family for so long it was hard to now see them as anything else. They'd come together and rallied around him as their own. *You're a part of this family, no matter what has happened,* Colleen had said.

But Colleen had also admitted to being at least partly responsible for what was happening. Despite Markus' assertions, Jacob wasn't convinced they could so neatly blame the dreamwalking. He knew Amelia's mind. It was strong, her will not so easily bent. It might be convenient, and hopeful, to blame something supernatural, but he recalled their last words together before she fell ill. Her heart was broken, but her mind resolved.

So why, then, would she book the plane tickets?

Everything Jacob would take with him fit into two small suitcases. Everything else sat along the curb of busy Tchoupitoulas Street below, awaiting pickup. Finding the wherewithal to part with this life was hard, but somehow the years with Amelia had given him a strength he'd not realized he possessed.

It was Amelia who had convinced him to renew his Irish passport several years back. He'd done it once as a teenager, at the prompting of Sister Agnes, but after he started a new life with Amelia, he wanted to put that chapter behind him entirely. *But it will always be a part of you,* she had said. Their subsequent trips to Ireland were an effort, on her part, to help him form new, happier memories of his old home.

A current passport would make relocating to Dublin a much easier matter, as a dual citizen of The Republic of Ireland and The United States of America. He could surely transfer his PhD work, but he didn't mind starting anew, either. The steps he'd taken in the States would pave the way for his new life back home, with his people. Perhaps he'd even look up some of his mother's family in Shannon.

All these things he considered without emotion. There was a decided lack of enthusiasm to all of it, his drive coming from a place of acceptance, and pragmatism. Life would go on because it had to.

But the matter of the plane tickets wouldn't go away. And the ache in his knuckles reminded him he needed to solve the mystery, or find his answers in a less healthy way.

It wasn't difficult to find the number for Father O'Connor. Killianshire was hardly even a town, and the priest was the head of the one and only Catholic Church within its limits. Nor did it take especially long for the young girl to track him down, as the size of the chapel was hardly greater than Jacob's current living area.

"Aye, Jacob Donnelly, how many years 'as it been?" the

booming voice of Father O'Connor came through the speaker. "Surely enough you coulda called sooner!"

"Aye, Father, for that I'm contrite," Jacob apologized. "But I'll be seeing ya soon in any case. I'm moving to Dublin. I'll come visit and we can catch the years up."

"Are ya now? And what about yer lass there in New Orleans? Don't tell me ye gone and messed that up. She seems a good one, from the brief talk I had wit her. And ye know I'm a good judge of such things."

Jacob nearly smiled. "You are," he agreed. "And Amelia is why I'm calling now. You said you'd talked to her?"

"'Course I did, and I expected to be seein' ya both months past, presiding over yer joining in marriage," the priest chuffed. "I hope yer callin to set a new date."

Jacob's heart dropped to the floor.

Marriage.

She meant to bring him home, to marry him with the woman who'd raised him at his side, and the one who'd saved him saying the sacred vows.

"Father, what did she say exactly, if ya don't mind?"

Father O'Connor dropped his voice. "I'm surprised to hear ye ask, lad. If ye two were in accord, you'd already know the contents of our conversation."

"Truth is, Father, something happened," Jacob ventured. "And I'm seeking answers. I promise to tell you the whole story when I return, but I hope you can help fill in some blanks for me."

The old man sighed, a sound of worried consternation. "Son, she called me quite serious one day asking to book the cathedral for your wedding. When I told her it was customary for the man to do the askin' and the bookin', she told me she wanted to surprise ye. That she meant to right a wrong. She also ha' me book the old Killian Castle for ye two, for the reception and honeymoon. Had it all squared and ready for yer arrival, and then the two of ye never showed. Sister Agnes was beside herself."

It was confirmed, then. All of it. Amelia's mind *had* somehow changed, and just nights before she fell ill.

And then it changed again.

Entirely.

"I appreciate you telling me," Jacob answered.

"You're as a son to me," the priest replied. He dropped his voice, which grew muffled as if covering the phone. "Yer meant for big things. Bigger than you can fathom, though beyond tha' I'll say n'more. When I pulled ye out of tha' house, t'was more than a twist of fate. And even so, ye fought hard enough for yer life tha' day. Don't give up tha' fight quite so easily now."

"When have you known a Donnelly not to fight?" Jacob replied, distantly, his mind already grasping the fact he wasn't likely to be leaving tomorrow after all.

16
OZ

Oz was in the kitchen preparing coffee for Amelia when he saw her rise for a stretch on the back porch. As her arms reached above her head, her sweatshirt revealed a glimpse of her stomach, eliciting thoughts of what the rest of her might look like in a state of undress. He swallowed, and went to deliver the coffee.

"Sleep okay out here?" He passed her the steaming mug, which she accepted gratefully.

Amelia nodded, taking a careful sip. The snarls in her pale hair sparkled in the rising sun. Her blue eyes squinted at the invasion of light. "I slept better in this stiff wooden chair than my own bed lately. Go figure."

"Change of scenery, maybe," Oz offered. There was no appropriate way to tell her that having her so close, hearing her light sleepy breaths, watching the rise and fall of her chest, gave him the best night of sleep he'd had in weeks.

"I need to get moving," she replied, heading back toward the house with her coffee. "I'm going to *Ophélie* today."

"I'll come with you," he offered, following her into the house. "I'm thinking of helping Nic, too."

After taking a couple long swallows, Amelia rinsed the cup in the sink. His words paused her, and, still facing away, said, "I don't think that's such a good idea."

Oz approached, leaning against the sink. "I need this as much as you do. I can't go back to the same life, to the firm. To any of it, really. Something has to change."

Staring into the sink, she nodded, sighing. "I know."

He ventured a light kiss on her cheek. "Why don't you go get dressed, and I'll meet you on your porch in an hour? We can ride together."

Amelia nodded again, her thoughts a mystery to him as she left the kitchen in a daze.

AMELIA INSISTED ON DRIVING, A MOVE WHICH TOOK OZ BACK TO their high school days. She'd always loved her sports cars, handling them with the devoted finesse of one who would have been at ease with a racing career.

As soon as they hit the Pontchartrain Expressway, she down-shifted the Porsche 997 Turbo to fourth and blew by the other cars before settling into sixth, her expression never changing. Her movements were fluid and methodical at once, her wrist ebbing to and fro as she rolled through the gears.

A dozen thoughts rose to Oz's lips as a means of filling the silence, but her focus left him with the impression she wouldn't welcome further intrusion. Her acceptance of him sitting in the passenger seat could best be explained as tolerance; at worst, a tragic complacency he'd thrust upon her with his ongoing insistence. It would mean little to explain his need to help Nicolas was sincerely more about him than her. That he hoped being close to Nicolas might also bring him closer to his repressed grief over Adrienne.

Things couldn't go on this way, but what that meant, exactly, was still beyond his comprehension. His sorrow for Adrienne would eventually spill forth, as it should. And even once healing had paved the way for moving on, Amelia's heart was not free... and really, did he want it to be? No matter how he might look to others, Oz knew there were more important things to be dwelling on than whether or not Amelia would ever return his affection.

By the time Amelia maneuvered the car on to the winding River Road, Oz had to fight to keep his breakfast down. She took even the blindest curves at speeds better suited for air travel, terrifying the oncoming drivers when she appeared out of nowhere, like a well-aimed bullet. As a teenager, she'd done this as a way of channeling her empathic angst. He could only assume this activity served the same purpose now, when her life was in complete disarray.

"You're turning into an old man, Sullivan," she teased with a brief, peripheral grin.

"Even if I wasn't afraid of dying, I can't imagine you'd walk away with your license intact if the parish deputies stopped us," he muttered, shifting straighter.

"Sometimes the distinct advantages to being a Deschanel actually *are* advantages," she reminded him, and then her expression returned to the same one she'd worn for the last forty minutes.

"I guess I can't complain, as you've managed to shave

almost a quarter of the time off the drive," Oz observed, as the white columns of *Ophélie* flashed into momentary view, behind dense foliage.

In a complete departure, Amelia politely maneuvered the sports car slowly down the long drive toward the Big House. Before they could knock on the giant oaken door, Richard appeared on the porch with a frown.

"Nicolas left with Mercy 'bout an hour ago. I don't know when to expect him back," the old butler apologized.

Oz cursed under his breath, but Amelia smiled. "It's no problem, Richard. We came out to survey the property. I'm mostly interested in the buildings out back, to see if they're still structurally sound. We're going to take a look around, if that's all right? And if Nicolas returns, you can point him in our direction."

Richard looked relieved at Amelia's amicable solution, and nodded before disappearing back into the mansion.

"What do we know about assessing a structure?" Oz raised an eyebrow as he followed Amelia's purposeful strides toward the back of the house, and the gardens.

"Nothing officially," she conceded, without turning around. "But I would like to understand what our capacity is, once the children arrive. *Ophélie* can house a fair number on her own, but as far as I understand, we don't have any inkling of a headcount. If we're struggling for space, we can look into constructing some pre-fab housing in the old sugarcane fields. We need to think about what our overflow situation will be, including hygiene facilities, and I *guarantee* Nicolas hasn't given it a passing thought." She frowned. "My mother started this work, before everything fell apart. I have no idea how far she got."

"The firm does a formal valuation annually," he offered, as they wove through Brigitte's Garden. "We can swing by the office on our way back into town and take a look."

"I already know about the estate audits," she replied, heading in the direction of the old slave cabins. "I had Rory fax me a copy two days ago. Several buildings may be of use, but the audit doesn't assess capacity or structural competence for housing. The blacksmith house, for example, can be cleared out as a small apartment for probably six, but I want to get a better visual. And I believe the slave cabins housed entire families, but we both know that was no humane way to live." She stopped, sighing in contemplation, adding, "But, we might not have a choice if they come to us in droves. God, I wish Nicolas was better about asking questions."

"You've given this some thought," Oz replied, impressed.

She turned to him, as they stood in the grove of old live oaks separating the gardens from the outbuildings. Her previously stoic expression had been replaced by a new, darker look, which scared him, though he didn't know why.

"It isn't some latent all-consuming passion for structural engineering, I assure you. You can accomplish a lot when you're determined to keep your mind off other things," she said, leaning against the thick oak, her hand resting upon a long arm that draped over the grass. "I can feel the threat of imperilment coming upon me sometimes, when my thoughts go too deep, or continue for too long. You know what happened last time. Strength means something different for me than it does for others."

Oz tentatively moved in toward her, stepping over the knobby roots. "I think it takes even more strength to experience pain and box it up, as you have to do. A special kind of strength I can't begin to understand."

Her eyes looked skyward. "I'll help Nicolas, because he's my cousin, and I love him. And because helping him deal with his grief will keep me grounded, and attached to my compassion without losing my head. Do you understand?"

Oz wanted to touch her. Her face, her hands. Her hair. He wanted to crush her pain, the way he always had with Adrienne, but it didn't work that way with Amelia. Giving her empathy only forced her to confront a pain that could make her ill. "I do. But why are you telling me this?"

Her hair fell over her shoulders, a wave of silver shimmer. "Because I can't be the same thing for you. It's more than knowing the feelings are wrong. It's a deeper warning... the seer's premonition... insisting, no *screaming*, for me to walk away."

Small gestures he'd never recall led to his next impulsive action. Before he reconciled the why, his lips were on hers, and his hands wound up and through her soft, silken strands as he pressed her into the tree with a potent desperation.

His heart surged when she returned the kiss, drawing him in a subtle, and inviting way. But the moment collapsed as she pulled her head to the side with a sharp inhale. "No," she said, simply.

"Why are we torturing ourselves, Amelia?" Oz challenged gently. "Our past is past. It's gone. Over. Done forever."

"Yes, I know—"

"*Forever,*" he emphasized. His hand settled on her hip, and she looked down at it with resigned puzzlement. "It's taken me years to understand this. Do you know how many damn years I dwelled over Adrienne, after she disappeared? How many other experiences I gave up, because I could not let go? Now that she's gone, I see it was always the outcome fate intended. I had agonized over something that was never mine, and now never will be again. I have to move on. *You* have to move on. And we both have to stop torturing ourselves over what we are feeling for one another."

Amelia watched him with a heavy silence. She nudged his hand away. "Is that what you think I'm doing? Torturing myself?"

"Isn't it?"

"I've understood all along whatever we're feeling is artificial. Not the result of a real, developing love, but of some unusual circumstances, or collusion of the universe. This isn't love, Oz." Her expression grew sad. "I'm sorry, but it isn't real."

"Just because we can't explain why or how, doesn't diminish the reality of what we are feeling."

"What you had with Adrienne was real. What I had with Jacob was real. *This* is a complication neither of us needed, and one that will inevitably destroy us."

The sinking, sick feeling in his chest felt like his heart breaking. Amelia's words merged in a horrible way with Papa Colin's warning. "All this time, I thought... assumed... you felt the same, and were trying to be the strong one."

"I do love you, but as a very old and cherished friend," she explained. "And as my friend, I care enough about you to tell you that you have to ignore these feelings, because addressing them will only lead to tragedy for everyone involved."

Yes, he was sure of it now. The darkness spreading through him *was* heartbreak. Somehow, he'd lost everything, and the one thing which felt real was something he'd either imagined or placed inappropriate importance on. "Amelia," he whispered, voice cracking as his chest caved, "I'll respect your position on this. But I wholeheartedly disagree."

He turned and walked back toward the house, before the sight of her pity could reduce him to unstoppable tears.

17
TRISTAN

Tristan groaned and rolled out of bed, falling back asleep on the way to the floor. He bumped his head and woke again, his alarm hurling warnings in his ear.

This was not unlike how he felt when he'd wake with a raging hangover, but there'd been no alcohol involved this time. He had, however, been up half the night with insomnia.

"You didn't eat dinner last night," Amelia scolded as he shuffled into the kitchen.

"Wasn't hungry," he mumbled.

"If my cooking is that terrible, you can tell me. I can take it," Amelia teased. Tristan smiled in spite of himself.

"The fact the neighbor's dog hasn't died from eating out of your trash must mean something," he bantered, as light-hearted as he could manage. He didn't want to seem ungrateful to Amelia, of all people.

"Maybe his senses are less finely tuned," she speculated with a laugh. "How are things at Magnolia Rest?"

"All right," Tristan replied with a shrug.

"What do they have you doing?"

"Looking after Jasper and Pandora's daughter."

Amelia stopped flipping the pancake and gawked at him. "Wait... they dumped Estella Broussard in a nursing home?"

"Estella? No, her name is Harriett."

Amelia gazed at the table thoughtfully. "I don't know anything about a Harriett. But their other daughter, Estella, is a real piece of work. One of the nastiest girls in all of New Orleans. Anyway, Harriet, huh? She must be the youngest. Are you sure you don't remember her from school?"

"I'm guessing we didn't run in the same social circles," he said grumpily.

"The Broussards are family."

"You didn't know who she was, either."

Amelia went back to the pancakes. "So what's Harriett's story? Is she sick?"

"I don't know her life story," Tristan snipped. He didn't feel like talking, and he couldn't help the annoyance creeping into his tone. "She's got a number of issues. Hasn't talked since she was a kid or something."

"Probably a seer or an empath," Amelia countered. "Wouldn't be the first to stop talking when things get hard. Aunt Maddy did that, according to Mom."

"Yeah, well, I don't know if she has any abilities at all," Tristan said. "And my job isn't to figure her out. It's to keep her company until my service ends."

Amelia sighed. "Okay, kid."

"What about you? Reconciled with Jacob yet?"

"Tristan—"

"Because you should. He's the best damn thing that ever happened to you. And did you know my mom even had dream premonitions about the two of you?"

His cousin laid the spatula down, bracing herself against the counter. "What are you talking about?"

"I don't know. She was convinced you and Jacob would save the family. Aunt C knows."

Amelia's head hung down over the stove, her expression blocked. Her left hand gripped the counter tighter to cease the trembling. His flippant reminder of her pain was needlessly cruel. His heart sank.

Tristan stood and embraced her from behind, laying his head between her shoulder blades. Her hands moved over his as she welcomed the comfort. "I'm sorry," he whispered.

"Not your fault," she assured him gently. "Now let me finish these pancakes, so we can get you fed and out of here before the cops show up and ruin breakfast."

TRISTAN PLOPPED DOWN IN THE PLUSH SEAT ACROSS FROM Harriett. She offered a quick, broad smile, and patted his hand, just like before, then returned to her window-gazing.

He eyed the books in his lap, wondering if it was even worth the effort. *She might not be all there. Shit, she might not even understand English. Maybe if she stopped speaking when she was seven, her development stopped there, too.*

Hell, maybe she does belong here.

Harriett kept her face turned toward the window, but

shifted her gaze ever so slightly in his direction. Then she winked at him.

The hell?

"Uh, all right, well, I'm going to read to you, if that's okay?" In response, Harriett closed her eyes and leaned her head gingerly against the window. The gesture was almost serene.

"*Great Expectations*," he said, showing her the cover. She flashed a polite glance, followed by a slight nod. He had no idea if that was agreement, encouragement, or merely a nervous tic. He decided it was easier not to analyze her likely meaningless gestures.

Tristan opened the book. Glancing around, satisfied no one was listening, he began reading aloud.

Despite his decision stop over-thinking her gestures, he couldn't stop. And each time, he'd imagine her nods or head tilts were encouragement to keep going, even though he knew better.

Around an hour into his reading, her soft breathing grew heavier and he realized she'd fallen asleep. He set the book down and slipped out to use the restroom.

When he returned, he found one nurse holding a squirming Harriett, and the other attempting to force something down her throat. Harriett thrashed and moaned, a sound that reminded him of a cornered animal.

"What are you *doing*?" he demanded, rushing over to the scene. Harriett's face was a splash of bright red. Tears poured down her cheeks. Her eyes held relief, but also something else. Pleading?

"Ms. Broussard needs... to... take... her... medicine!" said the nurse who wasn't holding her down, through clenched teeth. "But she's making this... unnecessarily... *difficult*!"

"Back off her!" Tristan positioned himself between Harriett and the pill-wielding nurse. The one holding her down didn't lessen her grip. "What are you giving her, anyway?"

"That's confidential," she grumbled.

"It's an anti-psychotic!" the nurse wrestling Harriett exclaimed. "Which clearly, she needs!"

"Or," Tristan countered, "perhaps she just needs people to stop tackling her to the ground and forcing things down her throat?"

The pill-nurse rolled her eyes, and threw the medicine down on the table, arms akimbo. "I didn't realize our community service reject had a medical degree! Did you, Helen?"

Helen shook her head. "No, but that's impressive indeed. Pray, tell us more about how to do our jobs, would you?"

Tristan considered reading their minds, but decided it wasn't worth the effort. "I have a few thoughts on the subject," he said, "but seeing as she's not real keen on your approach, why don't you let me try?"

The two nurses exchanged humoring glances and then both simultaneously backed away. "Oh, this should be good," the pill-nurse quipped.

Tristan knelt before Harriett, huddled in a ball on her seat, shaking. She peered at him through the crack in her hands. Her eyes were full of tears, splotched with red.

"Harriett," he whispered, ignoring the jeers and laughs of the two bully nurses. "Do you know what they're trying to give you?"

Suddenly, an image popped in his head. He saw Harriett being slapped and pushed by another girl. She looked like Harriett, but prettier. Despite her beauty, she radiated with pure evil. Another scene, the same girl holding Harriett down and forcing her to eat something Harriett was terrified of. It looked like one of the mud pies he used to make as a kid. *Where did this image come from? Who is the other girl, and how am I seeing this?*

Harriett... did you put that there?

And then, another image. The head doctor at the facility, Dr. Collins. Tristan was introduced to him yesterday, and he seemed as slimy as the facility he worked in. Slimy doctor was standing over Harriett's bed. He had one hand on her breast, the other in his pants. Harriett lay still, horrified.

Jesus Christ, Harriett. Are you sending me these images? Please, you have to give me a sign if you are. Anything.

Harriett squeezed his hand. Tristan gasped, but promptly squeezed her hand back, showing his support. *Well, now I know the answer to Amelia's question about the girl's abilities. But what is she exactly? Can she only project her thoughts, or is she reading my mind now?* There was so much Tristan wanted to ask, but it wasn't the time.

"Is playtime over?" Helen cackled, and the pill-nurse doubled over laughing.

"Harriet," he whispered again, ignoring them. "Put this in your mouth, and slip it between your back molars and your cheek. Pretend to swallow. Can you do that for me?" Harriett nodded, and Tristan's heart skipped again.

The nurses both watched in silent amazement as Harriett obediently placed the pill in her mouth, swallowed down the warm water in the Dixie cup, then opened to show it was done.

"Good," the pill-nurse said to Tristan, with snotty disdain. "You get to give her the pills from now on." The two fat nurses marched off, their laughter grating his soul.

When they were gone, Harriett spit the pill out into her hand. Tristan took it from her and slipped it in his pocket. "Don't worry. Do that anytime they try, okay?"

She nodded again. Tristan's heart leapt and his mind started to form words to all the unanswered questions he had. Then, without warning, she was gone again; her eyes glazed over and her head rolled sideways on her shoulders, falling into an unnatural nod. She closed her eyes, and within minutes was asleep.

18
COLLEEN

"Thank you for seeing me without an appointment, Aggie," Colleen said, as Augustus' secretary closed the double doors behind them.

"Heaven's sake, Colleen, you should know not to call me that when others are around," he grumbled as he moved toward his massive oaken desk. Colleen suppressed a smile.

"Humanity is an important, and often overlooked, aspect of a successful business," she chided, making no effort to hide the impertinence behind her words. From the time they were children, she'd always loved finding ways to goad her older brother. It was not easy to pull emotion from him, therefore a great and rare victory when she succeeded.

Augustus raised an eyebrow. "Let's recall where each of our strengths lie, and leave it at that."

"Do you have a new assistant?" she asked, taking a seat across from him. "I don't recognize her."

"Unfortunately," he groused, straightening his jacket.

"Marcy is on maternity leave. Our benefits are unusually generous, so I may never see her again."

"How lovely for Marcy! And I'd think you'd be less of a grouch about children now that you've become a grandfather," Colleen reminded him.

His mouth twisted. "Have I? I haven't heard from my daughter in months. Perhaps you're here to share news?"

Colleen immediately realized the error in her statement. None of them had heard from Ana regarding the birth of her son. The last news they had was when Tristan and Anne left Ana, Aidrik, and Finn to prepare for her final days before delivery. Too long ago. "I shouldn't have said that. I don't know if Ana is safely delivered or not. But you must know, it's not a personal affront. Ana loves you, Augustus. If it was safe to communicate, she would. Not even Nicolas has heard word."

"Not even Nicolas?" His laugh was bitter. "You say that as if it should give me some comfort."

Colleen saw no point in continuing the defense, and she equally knew her brother wouldn't want cosseting. Better to bring him back to a less emotional subject, and the reason for her visit. "I wanted to thank you for what you've done to help conceal Ashley's storms. Also for lessening the charges against Tristan."

Augustus nodded. "Ashley's behavior is not unwarranted under the circumstances, though it will be challenging, even for me, to continue holding the questions off if he doesn't stop."

"He knows that. I believe staying with Amelia is helping."

"As for Tristan... I get the sense there's some disappointment I wasn't able to get him off the hook entirely?"

"From Tristan, perhaps. But not from me, or Connor for that matter. Just because we *can* bail our children out of their problems, doesn't mean we should. Tristan is hurting, but he must learn some self-control or he'll never take accountability, and grow into a man."

Augustus digested that. "I might have done it anyway, if I could... the least I could do for Elizabeth. God rest her soul." He drew in a small, barely perceptible sigh. "But this was no simple matter of persuasion. I can convince a judge. Steve Cutler was nothing to persuade. Money alone would have done it for him. But the entire city was watching, and we cannot draw more attention on the family."

Colleen smiled. "Brother, I agree. You don't need to explain yourself."

He folded his hands over the desk. "You didn't need to trouble yourself coming all the way down to thank me, either."

She leaned forward, straightening. "That isn't why I came," she replied. "I need to talk to you about persuasion."

A small smile appeared on her brother's face. "Oh? Do I need to pacify another judge? This might be a new annual extortion record."

Colleen couldn't help grinning at her brother's infrequent, and somewhat awkward, attempt at humor. "No, though I'm sure the opportunity will arise again before the year is out, at the rate things are going," she assured him. "It's Amelia. I have a suspicion someone has used persuasion on her, but I have no way of detecting it other than my feeling on the matter. And..." she paused, realizing this next revelation might earn her another eyebrow. "Jasper suspects it as well."

She was doubly rewarded, as Augustus raised both brows in response. "I won't touch the Jasper comment," he answered. "But why do *you* suspect it?"

Colleen spent the next few minutes relating the weird behaviors of both Oz and Amelia since her daughter awakened. "Jasper suggested—yes, yes, I know, stop giving me that look—that it sounded as if both may have been put under the sway of persuasion. And as much as I'd like to disregard that possibility, the more I consider the anomalies, the more sense it makes."

"I agree, this behavior is very unlike Amelia." He reached for the mug to his left, drawing in a swallow of black coffee. At this time in the afternoon, Colleen guessed it was his fourth or fifth cup. His only vice. "And I've known Oz since he was a boy. He takes after his father. Which is to say, he has a strong code of ethics."

"I agree, with all of that," Colleen replied.

As Augustus watched her, she could almost see his thoughts churning. "You're starting with the wrong question, Colleen. What you should be asking is, why? Why would anyone persuade the two to such an irresponsible conclusion? To what gain?"

She considered Anne's retelling of the conversation with Nicolas, and his final words with Adrienne. Adrienne, who had struggled at being a wife and mother despite her longing to excel at both... who was now gone, and had known she was going, long before she breathed her last.

It was a long shot, but Colleen asked anyway, grasping

for missing pieces of the puzzle. "Adrienne didn't come to see you before she passed, did she?"

Augustus shook his head. "I hadn't seen her in months, in all truth. March, perhaps, when Nicolas had that function at *Ophélie* to introduce us all to Mercy."

Augustus would've told me. Coy is not his game, and, anyway, he would never have agreed to something he knew would cause such grief.

Her brother had always been exceptionally good at connecting dots, so it was no surprise he did so here. "You suspect Adrienne is behind this," he concluded. "A means of leaving her family in good hands, in a manner of speaking."

It was not until he spoke the words aloud that a fuller picture materialized for Colleen. "Yes… maybe. It wouldn't be unlike Adrienne to attempt something noble, but why Amelia? The cousins loved one another, and I can't imagine Adrienne would ever want to cause Amelia suffering."

Augustus stood and leaned against the large windowsill. Behind him, Canal Street was alive and bustling, while farther out the Quarter still rested at this early hour. "I can't claim to have understood the inner workings of Adrienne's mind. It was always a fragile, volatile place that escaped my comprehension," he said. "But perhaps you're viewing this from the wrong perspective. Rather than seeing this as a slight against Amelia's wishes, if Adrienne sought to protect her family, who better to do so than the person she admired most?"

Colleen realized her visit to Augustus was for more than an education on the inner workings of persuasion. His simple, yet powerful outlook on the human condition was uncanny. Her world was colored with complexity, and dimension. His was comfortably neutral. And sometimes the correct explanation was the simplest one.

What he suggested about Adrienne's motivation wasn't something Colleen could ever have attempted herself, even in her worst moment of desperation, but when she considered Adrienne's ever-delicate state, it was no longer so far-fetched. Perhaps Adrienne even felt Amelia's breakup with Jacob justified things.

"Can you reverse it?" she asked hopefully.

"Not I," he replied. "I can only reverse a persuasion I've initiated myself. It must come from the originator, as only they know the exact means used. I could counter it with my own, but that would only cause new problems."

"How am I supposed to find the originator, when the only person who had that knowledge is no longer with us?" Colleen lamented.

Augustus leveled his gaze on his sister. "Business, perhaps, is not your area of expertise. But your resourcefulness is nothing to make light of," he complimented. "You're the leader of a collective that catalogues abilities amongst our family, Colleen. You're in possession of a list of anyone and everyone who has this power. Use it."

"The Deschanels aren't the only powerful family in New Orleans," she countered.

"A fact few know," he reminded her. "If this is indeed Adrienne's work, it conveys an expected lack of elegance. She would've reached out to someone she knew. Her world was not as large as ours."

Colleen nodded. He was right. Adrienne would not have possessed the knowledge to go outside the Magi Collective, and that meant she must have reached out to someone within... and if she had, then Colleen would seek out every last illusionist in the family until the person was found.

"Thank you," she said, standing. "I suppose I could've reached some of these conclusions on my own, eventually. But as usual, your level head was a welcome help."

The smile on her brother's face in response was unusually earnest. "I'm grateful we also have a warm heart, in you. This family needs a balance of both." As quickly as it appeared, the smile faded and his expression was once again all business. "If you experience troubles with this illusionist, whomever he or she may be, feel free to call upon me again. I'll run intervention, if needed."

Colleen turned back toward her brother as she approached the double doors. "I appreciate that, but likely not necessary. A protective mother has some natural powers of persuasion," she said. She paused before adding, "And Augustus... Ana loves you very, very much. She knows everything you did, and still do, to keep her safe. All you did to fill the void left by Ekatherina. She was heartsick over the way you two parted in Maine. Don't take her silence as any more than vigilance for the safety of her child and family. I truly believe we'll have word of them soon. She would never turn her back on her father."

Augustus considered her words, saying nothing. With a curt nod, he returned to work.

19
JACOB

When Jacob assured Father O'Connor he would fight for Amelia, he'd done so without a clue of where to start. While he accepted the dreamwalking might be to blame, her unwillingness to sit down and discuss it posed challenges.

Colleen and Ashley existed as silent allies in his quest to mend fences. He only need say the word, and they would spring forth and assist. But this was Jacob's battle to fight. And he was ready to fight it, once armed with a few last trickles of information to better help him understand his invisible opponent.

There was one person he'd avoided speaking with thus far.

One at the heart of the entire situation.

. . .

Jacob sat across the table from Oz Sullivan, both staring into their mugs with the awkwardness of undiscovered discussion.

"Markus told me about the dreamwalking side-effects. Assuming you also know," Jacob asserted.

Oz nodded. "I know the theory."

"You seem skeptical."

"Because I am," Oz replied, drumming his knuckles against the wooden table. "I've never been easily compromised. I don't believe my mind could be pushed into feeling something I don't feel."

Jacob tensed his jaw. "What are you saying, then? That you love her?"

Oz dropped his gaze, gripping the ceramic mug with both hands. "It's not as simple as that."

"I'm capable of understanding complexity. Try me."

The other man sighed, the weary sound swirling between them in the tense air. It was evident he was broken, though the source of Oz's pain seemed, shockingly, not centered on the loss of his wife. "I know... wow, *do* I know anything anymore? I know what I feel for her is *real.* I don't know why I feel it, but it's not artificial, or the result of some dreamwalking sequence. She's all I can think about, every second of every day. I know I shouldn't. I've lost everything, and yet, feel nothing except where Amelia is concerned. When she's not with me, everything aches, from my head to my feet, and all I can think about is how to find a way to be around her next. I've never felt this way about anyone, not even Adrienne." He quickly looked up, guilt swimming in his tortured gaze. "You shouldn't have to hear this. I shouldn't have said any of that... I'm sorry."

Jacob's heart had first slowed, and then sped up to an unhealthy clip as Oz's desperate words tumbled out in a heap. They had the ring of deep infatuation, not some secondhand symptom from Oz walking around in her head. And if Oz felt this way... "What does Amelia think?" It ate at him to ask Oz, of all people, what Amelia was feeling.

Oz tilted his head, watching. "Is that why you're here? You think she and I are together?"

Jacob drew back. "I don't know what to think. And if you are... well, I suppose it's not my business anymore what Amelia does." His shoulders itched; knuckles ached. *Ignore it. You're better than this.* "But I have a lot of unanswered questions right now, and I suppose I'm not one to leave things unsettled."

Oz laughed, though there was no humor in the sound. "You can rest easy, then. She's done everything she can to avoid me." He sipped his tea, slowly, hands shaking. "She's doing a better job at fighting it."

"I won't bother you anymore about this," Jacob said, as he rose.

"She didn't choose me," Oz mused, hands trembling harder as his tea tottered against the wood grain. *The man is a complete mess.* "I know, not much consolation when she didn't choose you either, right? What I'm saying is, she's chosen to be alone. She can't stand the sight of me, and she can't bear the pain of your presence. But she shouldn't be alone, not after all that's happened. I worry about her constantly, and all I want to do is—"

Jacob raised a hand. "Maybe it's best you don't finish that sentence," he said, and moved toward the door. "Thank you for the tea, Oz."

Oz's demeanor was dreamy, faraway. His words had a languid, drugged effect. "We never… we were never together. You should know that."

"I already do."

"How?"

"Because Amelia said you hadn't, and I'll always take her at her word," Jacob replied, nodding at his once-friend before leaving.

He'd learned nothing of use. And yet, this lack of knowledge directed him forward.

Jacob, there's s' much I need to tell ye, his mother said, a month before she died. *But it isn't my place to reveal these wonders.*

I don' understand, Mama.

Your life has meaning beyond anythin' ye can imagine. Not in the way mine does, or yer father's. Or yer siblings. In a much bigger way. I fear you'll never know it.

Mama…

You're a Quinlan, Jacob. You were born Cianán Jacob Liam Donnelly. The words form s' much more tha' a name, son. I'll never get to explain it to ye myself, but someone will. Aye, I've already decided who.

Yer confusing me, Mama.

One day, Jacob. One day. All ya need to know is one day you'll meet another who makes yer heart soar. Ye'll know her when ye find her. Ye never let go of her, Jacob, no matter wha' obstacles are thrown in yer path. The fight in ye is bigger than yer fists. For 'tis more than love driving ya. It's s' much more. It's greater than anything you can see wit' yer own eyes, or feel wit' yer hands.

Mama, yer speaking silly.

Most of time, yes. But no' now. Hush. Remember these words, Cianán. Little ancient one. For there may come a time when they are all ya remember of me. Will ya remember?

Aye, Mama.

TEN MINUTES AFTER LEAVING OZ'S, JACOB STOOD BEFORE COLLEEN and Noah, his expression earnest, his heart full. His mother's words burning in his chest. He removed his tweed flat cap, pressing it over his chest as his heartbeat pounded blood through to each of his excited and terrified limbs.

"Mr. and Mrs. Jameson, I love your daughter, with all my heart. I couldn't walk away, even if I tried, and I won't, because it isn't in me to not fight. She's a part of me, and I'm a part of her. I don't believe Amelia is herself right now, and I know you've seen it, too. Whatever the cause, I can't believe it isn't reversible. Help me, to help her. Help me fix her."

Both Colleen and Noah pulled Jacob in for a crushing embrace. *You're a part of this family, Jacob, no matter what has happened.*

Noah stood back and beamed. "I knew it was you all along, Jacob. You're worthy of Amelia, but more importantly, she's also worthy of you."

Colleen added, "And your timing could not be more perfect. I know what's troubling her, and, now, I know how to fix it."

20

TRISTAN

Tristan woke an hour before his alarm went off, dressed, and headed out the door before Amelia and Ashley were up and moving around.

His thoughts were on Harriett. Her quite gazes, and measured gestures, giving him an odd sense of hope. He knew absolutely nothing about her, nothing beyond the gossip of her cruel nurses. He had so much to ask her, and feared he'd never get the chance.

Tristan hadn't thought of having a drink in days. He didn't know if it was Harriett's influence, but it was a nice feeling. Thinking back on how he'd acted during those dark days was horrifying. Humiliating. Even his words to his father were poison daggers to his ears. He didn't know how he'd lost himself so entirely. He had much to make up for.

Tristan stepped off the streetcar and walked down the avenue to the old brick building. There was a slight skip in his stride as he took in the fresh breeze and sauntered up the stairs.

Tristan made his way to the reading room, but Harriett wasn't there. Frowning, he approached one of the nurses to ask when she'd be back.

"She's in lockdown," the nurse said, and went back to reading her romance novel.

"Lockdown?" Tristan repeated. "What is that, exactly?"

The nurse rolled her eyes and tossed her head up in one exaggerated move, resembling a bobble-head doll. "It means she had another episode and we locked her down."

"So, where can I find her?" Tristan pressed.

"Ya can't," the nurse said, and turned her chair around entirely. By the time Tristan was ready with a response, she was already ensconced in her book again.

Tristan focused on the woman's thoughts. *Why anybody comes to see that girl, I swear I don't know. The doctor needs to keep the damn girl locked up and throw away the key. Why, she's the only one in that basement, so perhaps they will forget about her and save us all the trouble...*

Tristan's jaw tightened as he pushed away from the Formica counter and sprinted down the hallway. He'd never been in the basement, but he recalled a dark stairway in the corner of the building, one pulsing with an energy not meant for the living and breathing.

He squeezed down the constricted stairwell. Halfway, the air already felt thicker, denser. There was a subtle smoky sensation, like old dirt getting kicked up.

When he reached the bottom, he faced a very narrow passage, painted black. There were no doors on either side of the hallway, if it could even be called a hallway, but at the very end was a small, dimly lighted square. He squinted his eyes, and the square took further shape: a small window, set into a large, steel door. *If that's where they're keeping that poor girl, damn them and their entire families!*

Tristan could see nothing, not even his own feet. He was afraid to run, though he couldn't reach her fast enough. He hobbled through the bumpy, rocky floor and then finally did run, tripping over things he couldn't see or comprehend. At last, the pale, white square grew larger and larger and finally he was standing at the steel door, gazing through the cloudy, dirty window. Harriett curled around herself, weeping in the corner.

"Harriett," Tristan said, firmly. Loudly. He didn't care who heard him. *Let them come.* "We're leaving."

She lifted her head. Her long hair shielded her face, but Tristan could see her eyes. The tears were gone. Her gaze was wide, firm, resolute. Relieved. She nodded, and then a slow, beautiful smile spread across her face. *Ahh, she is so lovely. How could anyone discard her like this?*

"Cover your face!" he yelled. "I can't guarantee there will be anything left of this door, or this room, once I'm done with it."

Tristan closed his eyes and focused, forcing his thoughts forward and outward. Like many Deschanels, he also had a touch of telekinesis, but rarely put it to use. It was unimpressive compared to his telepathy, and he was untrained. But he knew what others were capable of, with focus. *I can do this. I know I can do this. I am the son of Elizabeth, grandson of August, and a descendent of Brigitte. I can do anything.*

His rage guided him as he spread his arms. His fingers began to tremble, first lightly and then so fast they cut a fuzzy blur before his eyes. The door before him shuddered in response, and a tiny crack formed down the middle. The crack grew to a gouge as the door caved inward, the sound of bending metal crunching through his skull. Harriett shrieked in surprise.

The sweat poured from Tristan's brow. His hands shivered with the power. *A little more... a little more...* Then, finally, a sickening snap and a deep low roar as the metal rent in half and tumbled to the cement floor.

He pushed through the ragged tear in the door and rushed to Harriett's side. The color had drained from her face, but her arms went around his neck without question. He lifted her into his arms with little effort, marched out of the smoking doorway, and back down the dark passage.

On his way back toward the narrow staircase, he didn't stumble, or falter. He pushed forth confident, and resolved. For the first time in as long as Tristan could remember, his life had some purpose other than being the lonely, ignored boy who'd raised himself. *We're not so different after all, Harriett.*

As he burst through the staircase and back into the main hospital, several nurses and doctors rushed toward the source of the loud noises. When they saw Tristan, their slew of questions commenced. *Was there an explosion? Was it the boiler? A fire?*

"Out of my fucking way," he commanded, without looking at them. Power still quaked from his fingertips. His mind pulled item after item off shelves, sending them crashing to the floor in a cacophony of chaos.

Harriett buried her face in the side of his neck, and her warm breath sent shivers of strength down his spine. *You're safe now,* he thought, pushing the words from his own mind into hers. She exhaled softly, acknowledging the promise.

After the display in the lobby, no one followed him. The police would be coming, and he was fairly certain he'd violated his probation. He might even go away, for a long time. But Tristan didn't care. For once, his issues were small in comparison to the ones of another.

"Can you walk?" he asked, tenderly. She nodded, and he let her down slowly, as she straightened her gown. "We need to take the streetcar. Okay?"

She only stared at him. He didn't wait for a more formal response, guiding her quickly down the avenue. His breath leapt in his throat as he heard the low, dull rumble of the streetcar ahead. Throwing frantic glances over his shoulder, he shielded Harriett protectively. He heard voices, yelling, calling out, and he fidgeted in nervous impatience. *Come on, come on!*

And then the St. Charles Streetcar came to a shuddering halt before them. He tapped his feet, waiting for passengers to disembark. As he heard the voices coming closer, he pushed Harriett ahead, through the crowds, and onto the car. Once aboard, he turned and slammed the doors closed.

"Hey!" a man in a dark suit exclaimed. "This is my stop!"

"Take the next one," Tristan returned, and rushed to the back of the streetcar, taking a seat. Harriett stood, dazed and swaying in the aisle, so he slipped his arms around her waist and pulled her into his lap. She collapsed against him, exhausted.

It's okay, we're going to be okay, he mentally shared. For whatever reason, her mind was shut to him but his was an open book to her. He didn't fight it. He let her have free reign of his thoughts, unchecked.

I want to know who you are, he appealed. *I want to know you, Harriett.*

But, as usual, she said nothing. Instead, she nuzzled further into his arms, burying her face against his neck. His skin was on fire, but her hot breath sent chills throughout his body.

Minutes later, they jumped off the streetcar and, taking her hand in his, he pulled her down the road. A light drizzle had started and they ran, hand-in-hand, through the rain. Harriett stopped for a moment, jerking him backward. When he turned to see what had happened, he saw her fling her arms wide and lift her face toward the sky. She was smiling.

Tristan wanted to throw her over his shoulder and run to the house, thinking of the danger lurking, but he didn't. Instead, he slid both of his hands across her face, brushing her long, wet hair aside. She lowered her head, meeting his gaze. *You'll always be safe with me.*

"I know," she spoke in return. His heart jumped. At first, he wondered if he'd imagined it; if the hope in his heart had created the response. But then she did it again. *Fourteen years she's said nothing, and she chooses to gift me with her first words.* "Tristan, I know you. I trust you."

Harriett's mouth found his and he gasped as their lips connected. Her arms looped around his neck, twining through his hair and down his back. Her kisses were not those of a quiet girl with nothing to say, but of a woman with deep and unnoticed passions. He tasted her tears and the rain through their kisses and this only incited him more. *I want you with me, Harriett. I don't know what this is, but I don't want you to leave my side.*

Then I won't.

Knowing their time was limited, he reluctantly pulled away, bringing an end to the first happy moment of Tristan's adult life. This time it was Harriett who ran ahead, sprinting like a track star toward Amelia's house.

Wait! You don't know where we're going!

I'm a Deschanel, of course I know where we're going!

He chuckled and picked up his pace to match hers. She was nimble and quick, despite the long, white gown she had to hold up. When they reached the door, Tristan fumbled with the locks, hands shaking, before the door swung open.

We can stay here until we figure things out. Okay? Tristan implored her.

Harriett nodded, smiling. *We're safe here.*

21

AMELIA

Amelia arrived home to find Tristan, and a young girl about his age, sitting on the couch, both wearing looks resembling wild, cornered animals.

At first, Amelia didn't recognize the young woman, but her mind quickly pieced the mystery together. She smiled amicably at both, then calmly requested, "Tristan, can we talk a moment?"

Tristan reluctantly rose, flashing an apologetic glance back at his guest before joining Amelia in the kitchen. "What's up?"

"What's up?" She laughed at his feigned nonchalance. "That's Harriett Broussard out there, isn't it?"

His eyes filled with shock, then his expression evolved almost to a proud defiance. "I did what I felt I had to. You would have done the same."

"I can't confirm that without knowing what's going on."

Tristan then unfurled a convoluted story of Harriett's abuse, first at the hands of her mother and sister, and later by the doctors and staff at Magnolia Rest. Amelia listened patiently, with her usual heightened empathy, waiting for him to finish. "I might have done the same," she conceded, choosing her words carefully, "but I'm not on probation, and walking a very thin rope. Do you realize this will be seen as kidnapping, in all likelihood?"

Tristan's defenses bristled. "So, I should have left her there, to suffer?"

"No, you should have told me about this sooner. My mother and I both have connections to the medical community all over New Orleans. We could have investigated the facility, and helped her in a way that didn't put you in jeopardy."

Tristan shook his head. "I can't explain the sense of peace I have right now, Amelia. Saving her wasn't a choice, it was a need. That girl in there has given me the first sense of purpose I've ever known. When the Magi Collective sent me to Wales to help Ana, I had a flash of it, but then it was gone. Like a tease. With Harriett, it fills me from head to toe and I'm absolutely terrified of losing this feeling."

Amelia didn't know what to say to this. She sensed the genuineness of Tristan's words. They radiated from him in powerful waves... the first strong emotions she'd detected from him in years that were not somehow tied to grief or anguish. But the situation was convoluted and dangerous. There was so much they didn't know. "We're going to need to call Jasper," she cautioned.

"I know."

"Uncle Augustus isn't going to be happy about having to smooth yet another thing over."

He sighed. "Yeah. I know."

She reached a hand across the table, squeezing one of his. "I'll call my mother about the nursing home. We'll get that situation quelled for now, until we can sort things out."

"Thank you."

Amelia stood and kissed him on the top of his head. "Jasper will be worried sick when he gets the call from Magnolia Rest. I'll give you a few hours before I call him, but we can't leave him hanging. Ashley is out of town, so you'll have the house to yourselves."

Tristan stood abruptly and pulled her into his embrace, nearly crushing her. Even in the tight hug, she could feel his excited, terrified trembling. "I owe you one," he whispered.

"Seeing you happy, for once, is enough for me."

AMELIA STEPPED OUT THE DOOR AND ON TO THE PORCH, REALIZING she had no idea where she intended to go. Ashley was in Biloxi following a lead on his wife and sons. She could go to her mother's, but her feelings were too complex to tackle tonight. She needed relief, not turmoil.

Looking up, she watched Jacob's car leave from the curb in front of Oz's house. He didn't seem to notice her as he left in a hurry, nearly hitting a truck turning on to Seventh from Coliseum. Across the way, Oz watched her, his expression blank.

Amelia jogged across the street, joining him. "What was Jacob doing here?"

"He wanted answers," he mumbled.

"Answers?"

Oz shifted, leaning back against his doorframe, wearing the same expression he'd had on the long, quiet drive back into New Orleans: weary resignation. “He wanted to know if you were in love with me.”

“I hope you told him the truth.”

“I’m exhausted, Amelia. If you want to come in, you’re welcome to. If not, that’s fine, too.”

Guilt over how she’d shamed him at *Ophélie* weighed on her. She’d left him feeling irrational, and foolish, when in truth it had just been easier to marginalize the emotions than to face them. Safer, for certain. But in protecting herself, she’d hurt him, resulting in an emptiness which made her feel more terrible than the flawed feelings ever had.

“I’d like that,” she replied.

AMELIA LAY ON THE CHAISE LOUNGE, FEET DANGLING OVER THE TOP curl of the chair. She propped herself with one elbow and sipped whiskey with her free hand.

“I’m sorry for what I said before,” she began. This was unstable territory, but to not venture through it would prolong the hurt she’d caused.

Oz waved a dismissive hand. “You were right. It was a good reminder.” His words were nonchalant, but his relief was palpable.

There was more to be said, but safer to leave it alone, for now.

“Are Christian and Naomi any better?” she ventured, realizing she hadn’t bothered to ask before.

He nodded, swallowing hard. “My parents left with them this morning. For Disney World,” he explained. More thoughts streamed: *I should be there with them, experiencing these firsts.* "For two weeks."

Amelia smiled half-heartedly. "I know it's hard for you to stay behind, but this is good for them. Children grieve differently, and it's important they feel some normalcy when they experience a big loss." Taking a swallow of her drink, she added, "Sorry. I'll turn the therapist off now. Although... you can call me doctor now, I guess. My degree arrived by courier yesterday."

He shot forward. "Amelia! That's fantastic! We should be out celebrating! You've been working nonstop since you graduated high school. Hell, before that. I remember you taking all those college courses junior and senior year, too."

"Yeah," she said quietly. His thoughts again betrayed him; she felt him observe her throat ebb as she swallowed the rest of her drink, and then poured another.

"I told Jacob you and I were never together," he attempted, clearly an effort to offer her something soothing. "He said he already knew."

Amelia set down her drink and gazed up at the summer night. "Jacob," she breathed, voice full of painful insight. *I've loved you forever, Amelia.* How long would this ache hold her underwater? "It's time for me to do something. I'm going to *Ophélie*... I can't keep putting it off. I mean *really* go. Sell the house. Pack my bags and never look back."

"You should," he agreed. Again his emotions were an open book, as the thrumming in his chest revealed his fear of seeing her less. She realized she shared that fear.

"The scientist in me is curious about the Empyrean children," she admitted, reaching toward the sky, grasping at stars. *She's drunk,* Amelia heard Oz think. He was right. "I want to help them, and study them at the same time. Markus wants to work together, to maybe discover a reprieve for our Curse in the middle of that understanding."

"You know my feelings," he replied. "No time spent trying to fix this is wasted time."

Amelia studied the constellations as if they carried an even deeper mystery than the one afflicting her family. Perhaps an answer to the seer's dreams which were both so innately familiar and yet entirely beyond her grasp. "I knew you would say that."

"Because you know me. Maybe better than anyone," Oz answered, his unprotected thoughts adding, *Even Adrienne never knew me the way she wanted to believe she did.*

"Ah, yes, I know you. You waltzed into my dreams on your great white steed, and rescued me from my own self," she mused, as her tongue mindlessly traveled over her bottom lip. "And no matter how much I work to convince myself to keep away from you, inevitably here I am."

The electricity in the air sparked, as it sometimes did when a Deschanel's emotions reached their summit. Oz knelt before where her head lolled back, gazing at her upside down smile. His own inebriation gave him the courage to slide his palms across her soft cheeks. Her eyes closed, as she drowned out the night sky and stars with darkness.

Her lips parted to speak, to protest his closeness, and she felt his willpower drain away. He pressed his mouth to hers, as he breathed her in. *Amelia, you're the only person on this earth who has ever been far enough in my head to fully get it.*

Oz moved his hands down past her shoulders, over her breasts and stomach, sliding under the waistband of her sweats. Her hips arched slightly, all the permission he needed to slip his fingers under the elastic of her panties and down further, where she was already growing wet. Months, since the last time she'd experienced intimacy. Since Jacob had run his strong hands across her, eliciting devotion and pleasure in a single gesture. *Then love me forever.*

When her hand came over Oz's to guide him in, his groan made him buckle, and she realized any control he had over himself would soon be lost.

More of his thoughts streamed forth: *I want to be the cause of her pleasure. The beginning and the end. For her to shudder beneath me.*

Her own followed: *I need to feel something. Anything. Anything but this irreparable loss of who I am and want to be.*

She slid herself into a sitting position then turned, wrapping her arms carelessly over his shoulders, draping them down his back as she deepened the kiss.

Oz stood, lifting her as he did. Her legs came around his waist naturally as he cupped her ass with one hand, moaning into her parted mouth. Their kisses grew evermore desperate as he set her atop the railing.

He had her sweats and panties off in one move. But in the next moment, he was stumbling backward from Amelia's push. Her eyes filled with panic as she scrambled to collect her pants. *He is not Jacob. Not Jacob. Not Jacob. This is not the way, not this.* "God, Oz, I'm so sorry. We can't do this."

Oz took a deep, stabilizing breath, and went to help her. "I didn't realize, I thought you wanted..."

"It wasn't my head I was leading with," Amelia lamented, as she struggled into her sweats, panties stuffed carelessly into a pocket. When she looked up again, her tears had won. "My heart aches so bad. I just wanted to feel something other than emptiness."

"I know the feeling," he whispered as he kissed her hair. "And I wasn't leading with my head, either."

"Something has to change," she said, into his chest. "Not eventually, but now. We can't just keep saying it. We have to mean it."

"Come on, let's get some rest," Oz said, pulling away and offering his hand. The look she gave him was skeptical, even when he assured, "Not like that, I promise."

Amelia paused, considering the promise she'd made Tristan. The call to Jasper could wait until morning. "Can I use Naomi's room?"

The disappointment in his expression appeared, and disappeared, in a single moment, replaced by a weary smile. "Of course. I'll grab you an extra pillow."

Amelia fell asleep to the memories her heart produced. Of Jacob. Of a love that felt like an eternity ago in time, but had dulled not even slightly in her heart.

Síoraíocht, a stór.

Tomorrow. It all changes tomorrow.

22
TRISTAN

Tristan listened in agony as Harriett poured the entire sordid story out to her father. Jasper took some time to catch up, clearly stunned at hearing his daughter's voice for the first time in over fourteen years.

Tristan was honored to have been the first she spoke to.

She was careful in her delivery of the abuse received at the hands of her mother and sister. *He'll never see them for who they are,* she explained to Tristan as they lay in his bed, the night before. He hadn't touched her beyond a few tender affections, both wound too tight from recent events to consider anything more intimate.

You don't have to go back to that house, Harriett, Tristan conveyed to her now, as she relayed everything to her father.

I know. But I will, for now. Look at how he suffers. He's always loved me, and will protect me now that he knows.

I *can protect you.*

You'll get your chance. Not so long from now, either.

She was a seer, so he assumed her words were prophetic. But Tristan had lost too much to trust in anything, anymore.

Trust in me, Harriett soothed. *As I trusted in you.*

"Harriett. My baby," Jasper lamented, burying his face in his jeweled hands. "This is my responsibility. I should have gone with your mother to check out the facility!"

"No, Father. You couldn't have known. They put on a great show for Mother. She was fooled as well."

That's a damn lie! Why are you defending her?

Harriett inwardly sighed. *To give him the truth is to hurt him irreparably. Half our comforts in life are illusions. Would you shatter those for someone you love, for your own gain? To be right?*

"I'll castrate the doctor myself, and see his practice burned to the ground!" Jasper exclaimed, fumbling, and failing, to retrieve his phone from his pocket.

"Amelia and Colleen are taking care of that," Harriett said pleasantly, reaching a soothing hand toward her father.

Jasper's eyes held a scattered look as he tried to settle on a thought. His gaze fell on Tristan. "You," he said. "Tristan, I thank you. When you sat before us earlier this year, swearing the Collective vows, I didn't know what your future held. I see now you have the heroic heart of your grandfather, August. A fine, fine man."

Harriet slipped her fingers through Tristan's. "He saved me." *In every way possible,* she added, for Tristan only.

Jasper observed the affection between them, lifting a tired brow. "Distant relation, I suppose nothing to get fettered about," he muttered, in a disconnected fashion. "I never thought I would hear your voice again, sweet pea. Do you know how lovely it sounds?"

Harriett's smile lit up Tristan's heart. "I didn't know if I'd ever find it again. But I did, thanks to Tristan."

Jasper nodded at Tristan once more in gratitude, then stood. "We should get you home, and into your own clothing."

When Harriett also stood, Tristan's heart surged. He hadn't thought about this moment, where he would be parted from her, even temporarily. The high caused by her presence began to recede.

"I'll meet you at the car, Father," she said, and Jasper glanced at the young couple once more before nodding and heading out the door.

Tristan was ashamed over the tears which formed in his eyes, and erupted, quickly spilling over. Harriett laid kisses against both eyelids.

"We have a purpose, Tristan. *You* have a purpose, one larger than even your huge imagination could ever envision," she said gently, touching a warm hand to his face. "Make amends with your father. As I will make amends with my mother. We do these things for ourselves. So we can close one chapter, and begin the next. Do you understand?"

Tristan nodded, feeling foolish for his emotions.

"I love you," she concluded, delivering the words through a tender kiss. "What we are is only just beginning."

Tristan watched her move down the stairs toward her father's waiting car, a jumble of aching sadness and tentative hope.

HE DIDN'T REALIZE HE'D BEEN WATCHING THE CLOCK UNTIL A knock sounded on the front door. *An hour. She's been gone an hour,* he noted, shuffling toward the door to answer it dutifully, as the only one home.

Aunt Colleen and Jacob stood before him in agitation, another woman in reluctant tow. She had the guilty, frenzied look of someone being booked for a crime. Tristan eyed her closely. *One of the Guidrys. Lougenia, is it? What the hell?*

"Where's Amelia?" Jacob started, as he entered the house without invitation. He didn't wait for an answer, bolting up the stairs.

"She's not here," Tristan told Colleen, as Jacob was already out of earshot. A part of him was overcome with curiosity, but his exhaustion overpowered it.

"Where is she?" Jacob demanded from the top of the stairs.

"She left early this morning with some bags. She took Miss Kitty, too. Her note to Ashley and me said she'd gone to *Ophélie*."

Colleen nodded. "Then we'll drive to *Ophélie*," she resolved. To her left, Lougenia stared at her nails with growing interest. "And come back to tend to Oz, later."

"Screw that. He's coming with us," Jacob concluded. The man flew down the stairs and past Tristan, nearly knocking him over in his rush.

Lougenia quietly shuffled back to the car. Colleen stayed behind a moment, noting Tristan with a curious expression.

"Something is different about you."

"Is it bad?"

She smiled. "No, darling. Quite the opposite. We'll discuss this later. Right now, I have to tend to Amelia's well-being."

Colleen embraced him quickly, and left.

23
OZ

Oz awoke late, and to the sound of fists hammering on the front door.

He shuffled to the window groggily, peering out at the street below. A long town car sat across Seventh, in front of Amelia's cottage. *Colleen,* he deduced, though it was not her fists splintering the wood.

A quick peek into Naomi's room revealed Amelia had already left.

By the time he made it downstairs, wearing flannel pants and a robe, the pounding had increased. Outside, Colleen good-naturedly scolded someone.

Oz should have put together that Jacob would be standing before him, once again, but his sleepiness put him at a disadvantage.

"Get dressed," Jacob commanded, before Oz could issue a greeting. He glanced at Colleen, but she looked to Jacob in a strange deference.

"It's nice to see you, as always, Jacob," Oz muttered,

widening the door. But Jacob didn't step through. "If you're looking for Amelia, she left sometime before I woke."

Oz only realized the fault in his words after they were out.

The fire on the Irishman's face surrounded him in a terrifying halo. Colleen's hand instinctively latched to Jacob's arm in a flash, cautioning. From the corner of his eye, Oz could have sworn he saw Jacob's hand twitching, and, in tandem, his expression at war with whatever violence lurked beneath. *Perhaps those rumors about his past are true.*

"We'll sort that out later," Colleen placated, with a smile even Oz could see disguised an anger that quite possibly matched Jacob's. "Oz, please get dressed. No need for anything of occasion. But please, with haste."

A pointed look traveled from Jacob to Colleen.

Oz wanted to ask more questions than his tired mind was ready to formulate, but understood the protective fury boiling inside Jacob would only grow with each moment he stalled. It went beyond his accidental admission of Amelia's staying the night. Jacob was clearly angry when he arrived, pummeling Oz's front door. As was Colleen, and *that* was something rare to behold indeed.

Even stranger, Oz thought as he hustled upstairs to get into something decent, it didn't seem as if their anger was directed at him.

TEN MINUTES LATER, OZ WARILY SAT IN THE BACK OF THE TOWN CAR with Colleen, Jacob, and a very contrite-looking Lougenia Guidry. What on earth a Guidry had to do with this unexpected party, Oz couldn't begin to imagine, but he supposed he was about to find out.

The car had been custom-fitted with the back two seats facing each other, limousine style. Colleen had diplomatically guided Jacob and Oz toward opposing seats, a wise choice Oz appreciated, though the energies coming off Lougenia to his left were unsettling.

"Don't think of it," Colleen soothed, placing a hand on Jacob's knee as it bounced in agitation. "It won't matter, soon. It will be as nothing."

Jacob responded with silence, but his eyes burned holes in Oz's soul.

"Oz, dear, we've found an end to your confusion," Colleen said, brightening. "It was no easy matter to uncover, but through the help of others, and Lougenia's cooperation, we believe we can reverse all that has been done." Her apologetic glance at Jacob seemed to add, *Well, perhaps not all.*

Oz shook his head. "I'm sorry. You're going to need to start from the beginning."

"Those feelings you have for Amelia... the ones you keep insisting are real?" Jacob cut in. "They're not."

Colleen flashed a placating smile at Jacob, and then said, "Initially, we all believed the residual feelings which transpired between yourself and my daughter were a result of the dreamwalking," she clarified. "An unfortunate side-effect. We now know that not to be true. The dreamwalking quite possibly did create a special bond between the two of you, but not one strong enough to overwrite your individual willpowers."

"I never thought it was the dreamwalking entirely," Oz

defended, "but the idea of my feelings being reduced to something artificial is frivolous."

"So, you think all those years you were married to Adrienne you were secretly in love with Amelia? That's bloody ridiculous," Jacob snapped.

"More importantly, false," Colleen once again pulled the conversation back to a pleasant exchange. "I conversed with Jasper on the matter, and he suggested this was the work of an illusionist. I confirmed my suspicion with Augustus, and then proceeded to cross-reference the list of illusionists on family record. Eventually, this path led me to Lougenia, who spilled before us a story so elaborate and unbelievable I'd have thought it a work of fiction if we hadn't already been embroiled in our own improbable situation."

At the mention of her name, Lougenia diverted her gaze out the window, her body language suggesting jumping out might be a viable option.

"I don't understand. Illusionist?"

"Illusionists manifest in many ways, as you may or may not be aware. The crux of this ability is one who possesses it can manipulate the reality of their target in some way. Markus, here, can affect the way others behold him," she explained, with a wave toward the front passenger seat. For the first time, Oz noticed Markus, who merely held up a hand in greeting, but didn't turn around.

"Others, like my brother, Augustus, can use their illusion to persuade others to believe what he wants them to believe. I'm sure you already knew about his specific talent, as he is sometimes called on as our family fixer. What you may not know is that Lougenia is in possession of the same flavor of illusionism as my brother."

"All right," Oz said, only a small piece of him beginning to sense the direction the conversation was heading.

"It gets better," Markus announced from the front seat.

"Worse, you mean," Jacob muttered, with obvious restraint.

"It took some persuading of my own to pull the story from Lougenia, but once I'd explained the damage before us, she eventually confessed," Colleen went on. "It seems Adrienne solicited her assistance before she passed."

"Adrienne?" Oz knew there were better questions, but repeating his wife's name was the only thing he could voice.

"Oz, darling, you know Adrienne has always loved you dearly. At times her actions were misguided, but they were always well-intended," Colleen prefaced, tentatively. "With that sentiment in mind, she sought out Lougenia's help providing for you, and her children, after her passing."

Oz grimaced. While he still felt numb at his wife's death, a frustration burned deep within him at the way she'd hid her illness, right up to the bitter end. "I'm capable of caring for our children without assistance."

"Of course," Colleen agreed. To her side, Jacob turned to watch the passing scenery, perhaps in further attempt to keep himself grounded. "It was not your estate Adrienne sought to protect. But your heart, Oz."

"She insisted y'all weren't together no more!" Lougenia burst out, leaning with intent toward Jacob. "Was s'posed to be clean! No one getting' hurt."

Jacob opened his mouth, then closed it again, drawing in a deep breath. Colleen's glance toward Lougenia was not unkind, but it *was* a warning. "Adrienne felt you couldn't survive widowhood a second time. Nor losing her, after all the two of you had been through over the years. She decided to pick a replacement, and that replacement was Amelia."

"That's insane. Adrienne would never do such a thing!" Oz protested, but even as he said the words, he grasped it was exactly the kind of thing his late wife would do.

"Insane or not, she did it," Jacob said pointedly. "And that's how we got where we are today."

"I know this comes as quite a shock." Colleen leaned across to place a hand on Oz's knee. "But now that we know, we can set things to rights. Lougenia has agreed to reverse the illusions she planted in both you, and Amelia. Once she does, things should return to normal."

Normal... what *was* normal anymore? His wife was gone. Really, truly gone this time, not simply disappeared as she had years before. His feelings for Amelia were the first real thing he'd recognized in some time, and now Colleen was telling him those, too, would be gone?

And if his feelings for Amelia did disappear—despite his faith in Colleen, Oz was not entirely convinced—would they be replaced, finally, by the grief he knew was festering somewhere inside him for Adrienne?

"I know this is a lot to absorb," Colleen acknowledged. "But if I wasn't positive, you would not be sitting across from us."

"Oz, buddy, you might put Jacob at ease if you looked a bit more relieved," Markus called, meeting his gaze in the rearview mirror.

"Relieved? I have no idea what to feel," Oz replied. "And I'm not convinced, either," he added with an apologetic glance at Jacob. "But what choice do I have?"

"None," Jacob confirmed. "If you still love her after, that

will be your problem to sort. But I know Amelia, and none of her behavior since she woke has been anything like her."

"Maybe you don't understand why she walked away from you," Oz ventured. "She's protecting you, and I don't expect that to change with whatever will happen this morning."

"I'll hear it from her lips, then, not yours," Jacob replied.

Oz said nothing. They were still thirty minutes from *Ophélie*, so he closed his eyes, and let his mind work through all the possibilities awaiting.

AMELIA SAT WITH A BLANK EXPRESSION AS SHE LISTENED TO THE same story Oz had absorbed on the ride over. Her already pale skin turned ash-gray, and her hands, clutched in her lap, were turning white.

Nicolas stood behind the tall chair she sat in, gripping the corners. "Fuckin' Adrienne," he breathed, in bemused wonder. "I thought she was rambling, like she always did."

"Not this time," Colleen said, with a tight purse of the lips.

Amelia's gaze drifted back and forth between her hands, and her mother, but her peripheral was trained on Jacob. She seemed intent on avoiding him.

"I cain't say sorry enough," Lougenia blubbered, kneeling before Amelia as if looking for penitence. "It wasn't s'posed to be like this."

Amelia reached a hand over Lougenia's, and smiled wearily. "I'm not angry with you, Lou. If Adrienne had come to me for help, I'm not sure I could have refused her, either."

"Let's get this over with," Markus asserted. "It's gone on long enough."

Lougenia asked for Oz and Amelia to kneel beside each other, in front of her. Oz caught Amelia's eyes for one, brief moment before she averted them again. *There's no way this isn't real. I know I love you.*

Don't I?

Saying nothing, Lougenia laid her hands gently atop both their heads. The tension in the room was so thick, Oz had the overwhelming urge to break out in song, simply to cut through the strain. Jacob leaned against the mantle, brows furrowed. Markus' crossed arms felt borderline authoritative, while, in contrast, Nicolas' cocky stance suggested cool boredom. Colleen, in a rare loss of control, seemed unaware she was chewing her nails.

In the background, the grandfather clock ticked, the only sound other than the anticipatory sighs and grunts trickling through the room.

At last, Lougenia stood, backing away. "It's done."

Colleen was the first to rush forward. She ran her hand lightly over the back of Amelia's hair, soothingly asking, "Are you all right, Mia?"

Amelia stared at the floor. She nodded. "I'm fine. Just feels like my breath was temporarily stolen."

Oz knew exactly the sensation she described, but in addition, he was consumed with a myriad of other feelings, most predominantly a keening ache for his children.

Then an acute, twisting pain in his chest as he realized, finally, Adrienne *was* gone. His spirited, impulsive, beautiful redhead was *gone.* And nothing, not any of this, or anyone standing here, or anything within their power, could bring her back.

Memories rolled over him in waves.

The first time they made love. *You'll come back?* he'd asked. *I love you, Oz,* she'd replied.

Perusing cheap tourist traps in the Quarter. *You're such a mystery,* he'd confessed.

Maybe that's why you love me.

Trust me, darlin'. Mystery is not a bad thing.

When her father sought to come between them. *Adrienne, I love you. I need you. I would never leave you. Never.*

Oz, don't let him do this. Don't let my father do this. Please.

I won't. Adrienne, please don't cry.

When he'd proposed in desperation. *Marry me!*

What did you say?

I said marry me, Adrienne. Marry me. I love you so much! Please, don't ever, ever think I don't. It hurts me when you say that.

Later that same night. *Oz, I cannot wait to be your wife.*

Adrienne Leigh Sullivan. It has a nice ring to it, doesn't it?

Eh, it'll do. Her beautiful laughter.

Later still, after years apart. *Oh, my Big Hero,* she'd whispered, against his neck as he made love to her, after believing her dead all that time.

Marry me, Adrienne. Once more.

Yes, Oz.

After learning he had a son. *I'm only Oz when I'm with Adrienne.*

A year ago, when life could get no better; no more wonderful. *Are you ever afraid?* she'd whispered. *Afraid I might disappoint you? That Naomi and Christian might disappoint you?*

Don't ever say that. Don't ever stop trusting in me.

I love you. I sometimes remember the things I've done and I have to remind myself you don't hold them against me. Forgive me, Oz.

I already have.

All at once, the stillness in the room was oppressive, choking him from his constricted throat all the way to his tensed feet pressing into the old carpet. He stood and pushed his way toward the hall, needing to be alone.

But before he could completely escape, Lougenia said, "Wait. I've somethin' else to tell y'all."

24
AMELIA

All eyes rested on their trembling cousin as she steeled herself to confess something that appeared to be eating her up inside.

"Go on, dear. No one will harm you here," Colleen urged.

Amelia caught a glance of Jacob who, for the first time since arriving, was not focused in her direction. The bruising around his eyes, nose, and jaw had improved, but was still a reminder to her of how he'd given in to an old weakness. She wasn't naïve enough to blame herself, but she understood she'd drawn on Jacob's strength all these years. When he needed hers, she wasn't there.

The ache for Oz had dulled. In its place, a genuine affection sat waiting. But how could it not, after all they'd been through? The three months he spent in her head made up an experience they could never explain, or share, with anyone else.

But she understood, with profound relief, that she was not in love with him. For the first time in months, her feelings were clear, and her thoughts lucid. She no longer felt captive to a mind and heart that didn't match.

Lougenia fixed her agitated expression on Amelia. "Y'all are wrong, 'bout what saved ya."

To her left, Jacob shifted. Oz stood in the doorway, listening. "Go on," Amelia urged.

"T'wasn't some nonsense 'bout lettin' someone go or whatever," Lougenia wrinkled her mouth. "I can't pretend to understand y'all's logic anyhow, but t'wasn't that. Adrienne saved ya, with that, uh, ability a'hers. Ya know, absorption?"

Colleen stiffened. "What are you talking about? Adrienne had the power of absorption?"

Lougenia nodded. "Ya. T'was how she got that brain problem o'hers to begin with. Took a headache or somethin' from her little girl, and it got all kinds of outta hand. Knowin' she was dyin' anyhow, she took all that blackness surroundin' Amelia and pulled it right into herself. I watched her. She was dead not an hour later."

"You're not making any sense!" Oz's yell shocked the room. "Adrienne *never* had any abilities whatsoever!"

Lougenia shook her head, prepared to rebut, but Colleen spoke first. "This is not surprising to me in the least. We know now that Nicolas wasn't benign at all, instead simply repressed by Aidrik's protection upon the heir's family. Once exposed to an Empyrean, Nicolas began to exhibit his own powers. Why would Adrienne not, then, do the same?"

"She would have told me," Oz insisted, shaking his head. "She'd never have kept such a thing from me."

"Yes," Amelia broke her silence. "She would have. Adrienne has been protecting you forever, Oz. Even you know this."

Lougenia shrugged. "I can only deliver the truth to y'all. Up to y'all what you wanna believe. Adrienne saved her daughter, and she saved Amelia. Hand to God."

Oz drew in a shaky breath and then disappeared into the hall. Nicolas followed.

Colleen knelt before Amelia, pressing the back of her hand against Amelia's forehead. "Are you sure you're all right? I've never seen an illusion reversed before. I forgot to ask Augustus about side-effects."

"I'm fine, Mom," Amelia vowed. "Please, go check on Oz. He's taken in some unthinkable news." *And it's not my place to comfort him... if it ever was.*

"Mia, there's something I must tell you," her mother pressed. "Before you make a foolish choice you can't take back!"

"Mom," Amelia smiled. "I promise, I'm not planning anything foolish."

Her mother watched her for a moment, waiting for evidence of something amiss, and then stood to oblige. Markus tugged on Lougenia's arm, urging her to follow. He offered Amelia a knowing look, as their departure left Amelia and Jacob alone.

She stood and faced Jacob, who examined her with a carefully blank expression. She sensed clearly his confusion and fear, both emotions radiating from him in powerful vibrations. *He's in limbo, waiting to hear me either tell him I love him, or to leave me be.*

Amelia offered her arm. "Wanna go for a walk?"

• • •

Their stroll took them through Brigitte's Garden. Amelia felt the warmth course through her the moment she slid her arm through his protective, strong hold. She sensed his strong, rapid heartbeat through the thin shirt.

She wasn't intentionally torturing him. Words failed her.

"I don't know where we go from here," she whispered, finally, stopping. "I've been so foolish."

"You're a part of me, Amelia," Jacob replied. He untangled their arms, then brought her hand to his heart, pressing it firm. "The most important part. And we've both had our moments of foolishness." He frowned, and the shadows caught the bruises coloring his jaw.

"I like to think myself more sensible than this," she said. "But I suppose I've been surrounded by paranoia and fear for so long, it finally penetrated. I should have known letting you go wasn't what really saved me, but it was a convenient thing to believe when it unburdened my conscience. To know you would be safe."

"You forget, I've a say in the matter, too," came his gentle reminder. "I know what's best for my own well-being."

Amelia nodded. "You're right. I never really let go, any more than you did. It's a big part of why I never gave into any of the weird feelings for Oz." She grimaced."Well, at least not entirely."

"There have never been secrets between us. Tell me."

"Last night I shared some whiskey and conversation with Oz. Things started to get out of hand, but I stopped it before..."

Amelia choked back a laugh at the immediate relief on

Jacob's face. His smile warmed her once more. "None of this was your doing."

"I never wanted to drag you down into this family, but my heart got the best of me."

"I know. As did mine."

"And then, I saw an opportunity to set you free, and I didn't even question it," she went on, with a sad sigh. Her hand traveled up and rested over his, as she looked up, her eyes imploring him. "But in doing so, I've completely disrespected your free will, and your role in this. It isn't my decision to make. You know the malediction of my family, and what it means to be a part of it. If you love me, and you still want this world, risks and all, then I'll stop pretending it's my decision to keep you away. If you still want me, I'm yours."

Jacob's smile turned the world upside down. "I've loved you forever, *Blanca*."

Her heart surged at the way his voice wrapped around *forever*, which had the lyrical ring of an eternity lived.

"Then love me forever."

EPILOGUE

Tristan

This was neither the first wedding he'd attended this year, nor the first castle he'd visited. In fact, the happiest moments from the year had come in the presence of a castle, and couples who belonged together, uniting their lives, separate strands becoming one unbreakable knot.

Unlike the last one—Ana and Finn's, in Wales—this wedding had more than its share of Deschanels in attendance: Colleen, Noah, and Ashley, of course, but also Markus, Evangeline, Anne, and even Augustus, with his wife, Barbara. Nicolas and Mercy were unable to come, but had instead insisted on paying for the entire lavish event.

Attendance on Jacob's side was woefully thin in comparison, though not lacking in enthusiasm. Sister Agnes couldn't stop gushing over the couple, and Father O'Connor's beaming smile as he led the vows was contagious to all.

It hadn't taken much convincing to get Harriett to come to Ireland as his date, though she was still understandably nervous after living half her life in quiet seclusion. Her home situation was beginning to stabilize, and Tristan almost hated to pull her away. *I want to do this. For you. For me. For us.*

For us... the words terrified Tristan, while also filling him with powerful hope. He feared letting that hope grow beyond his control, but after losing everything in his life, he understood you couldn't have love without the fear of loss. Harriett was only his so long as the universe allowed. But while she was, he would enjoy her as she enjoyed him, two young souls, misunderstood their entire lives, now whole.

Soon, they would join Amelia, Jacob, Oz, Markus, and Anne as they rallied around Nicolas and Mercy's cause. *It's happening, soon. I can fucking feel it,* Nicolas insisted, in his usual eloquent fashion.

"I've never seen happiness like that," Harriett mused, as Amelia joined Jacob at the cathedral altar. Candles burned around them by the thousands, the only light on this dark, magical Irish evening. "You know, they were meant to be together. I can't quite grasp the thread, but it's there. Their connection is old, and powerful."

"That's how happiness looks when you're with your heart," Tristan replied, gently squeezing her hand.

"I like that you have romance in you," she whispered back. "My father says it's a lost art."

"I don't really know much about it," Tristan confessed. He watched Jacob and Amelia exchange their vows, transfixed by the shared look between them. "But I would like to."

"We can learn together," Harriett promised.

Tristan supposed he should be concerned Harriett was his cousin. But a distant blood tie felt insignificant in the face of everything else he'd endured. He wouldn't give this feeling away for anything.

Two rows ahead, Tristan observed the gleam of joyous tears on his Aunt Colleen's face. The pillar of this family, she had endured the weight of everyone's grief in order to sustain them through the storm. She'd lost as much as anyone, and yet maintained the burden for others. After everything, she could now be part of her daughter finally taking her path to happiness.

When at last Father O'Connor announced Amelia and Jacob man and wife, the roar from the small crowd blew half the candles out. Jacob nearly crushed Amelia's smiling face in his strong, but trembling, hands, his electric kiss eliciting a knowing gasp from the onlookers.

Hand-in-hand, Amelia and Jacob ran back down the aisle, toward the large double doors leading out into the night. Together, they flung open the doors, both erupting into laughter created by something none of the guests were privy to.

After a respectable wait, Colleen and Noah fled down the aisle as well, enveloping the couple in a tangle of hugs, quickly joined by Ashley, Sister Agnes, and the remaining guests.

The wind rushed in, carrying the scent of grass and wood smoke. Outside, Tristan could see nothing except his loved ones, and the endless sky of stars.

Not so very long ago, he'd gazed up into a similar sky, with similar hope in his heart. Then his world had fallen apart, taking his hope with it.

"Your world is only just beginning," Harriett whispered, as she linked her arm through his and lead him toward the door, the outside, and a future full of possibilities.

Amelia

KILLIAN CASTLE DATED BACK TO THE FOURTEENTH CENTURY, A tower stronghold built as the Norman dynasties and fashions were in decline. Abandoned until the early twentieth century, it was restored by private trust, and then turned over to the village of Killianshire, for use only by residents.

As a child, Jacob had played around the hill leading up to the castle proper, pretending to sail his ships in the long-dried moat. He'd navigate up to the hill's base, and then scale the incline, demanding the lord of the estate release the fair maiden held captive. His rescue of the bonny lass would culminate in a wedding to unite all kingdoms, with long-awaited peace restored to warring clans.

All of this, Jacob confessed to Amelia years ago. They'd giggled about it then, but she'd never forgotten.

And now, she realized, his delightful child's imagination may have been more prophetic than anyone realized.

Perhaps Jacob had some magic in him, after all.

THE RECEPTION WAS A SIMPLE AFFAIR, AS FAR AS ANY RECEPTION held in an ancient stone castle can be simple, with fare chosen from what the lords and ladies would have eaten in its height of power. As with the cathedral, the stone rooms were lit with candles, and moonlight streamed through the open arched windows. A roaring fire burned in the hearth, a spit of lamb turning slowly above the flames.

The couple's first dance was a melodic, acoustic version of Foo Fighter's *Everlong. The song playing the moment I really saw you, for who you were,* Amelia had said. Jacob's reply: *How could I ever forget the shameless way you ogled me like a piece of man-meat, when I was minding my own business, perfecting my air drum solo? Hell, I finally got the bass drum to behave.*

After, the musical accompaniments took on a more classical feel, with local instrumental pieces picked out by Sister Agnes. The lively sound of fiddles, pipes, and drums would be forever embossed in Amelia's mind. Echoes of joy.

Her feet ached from hours of dancing, and her throat sore from exclamations of elation. When at last the hour grew late, her loved ones took their leave to the inn. Only she and Jacob remained, where they would later retire together under protection of the tower, their first night as a married couple.

With a keen intuition, Jacob lifted her tired feet upon his lap, her dress dangling to the side in an unladylike fashion. He started his massage from the heels, working up over the ankle, toward her calves. "You dance like an Irishwoman," he said, with a gleam of pride in his eyes.

"Aye, I spose tha's cos' I am now," she replied.

"I don't sound like that, Mrs. Donnelly," Jacob chastised, winking. "*Although,* you once told me it turned you on when my Irish came out."

"Oh, I told you that, did I?"

"You might have showed me."

"I've always been better at showing than telling."

Jacob's hand traveled further up her leg, passing over her knee, settling on the softest part of her inner thigh. "I'd tell you I love that about you, but I think I'd prefer to show you instead," he asserted.

Amelia gasped as he pulled her to his lap in one powerful tug. Filled with a rush of immediate yearning for her husband, she snaked her hand between his legs, but he surprised her by stilling the questing hand.

"No," he purred. "It's our wedding night, *Blanca.* Much as I'd love to rut with you like a wild animal, we should make it last. The witching hour will arrive on the half."

"*And*?" Jacob's restraint inflamed her desires further.

"And, are ye not a witch, lass?"

Amelia bit her lip, squeezing her legs tight against him. He emitted a tiny gasp, as his eyes rolled up. "You shouldn't tease a witch. You can't know what she's capable of," she countered.

"Oh," Jacob replied, face entirely earnest, "I know exactly what you're capable of, Amelia Donnelly."

She stood, backing away toward the door, her expression beckoning him to follow. As soon as he made to do so, she sprinted out the arched frame, and pattered down the stone steps, exiting into the cool night air.

"You'll catch a chill," Jacob warned, but was smiling.

"Catch *me*," she challenged, and then was off before he could say another word.

Amelia's natural quickness was slowed by the heavy dress, but the head start carried her well ahead of her groom, as she flitted first over a steep hill, and then disappeared into the dense forest.

She lost the sound of him after she was about a hundred yards in, and her natural sense of direction began to falter. Moonlight unable to penetrate the heavy tree-cover, shadows surrounded her from all sides, reminding her the wilds were as their name suggested.

Just as she decided to return, Jacob's strong arms encircled her waist.

"You can't best me in my own woods," he teased, but she silenced him with a deep, longing kiss.

"You've rescued your lady, Jacob. Like you always wanted."

He eyed her in bemused surprise. "You remember that silly story?"

"It's not silly," she insisted. "There's magic in my blood, and there may be in yours, too."

Jacob's hand traveled to her hair, which had come out of the Celtic knot, and he pulled it through his fingers, watching it fall in waves. "Silver and starlight," he mused. "The colors of magic."

"My mother told me a story this evening," she pushed on. She was nervous... even to tell Jacob, who would never tease her for who she was. But she believed it, and knew he would, too. *Mia, I tried to tell you this in the parlor at* Ophélie, her mother had said, as she helped her into her wedding dress. *I'm sorry I kept it from you all these years, darling. The story is rightfully yours, and now the prophecy will come to pass, as it was always meant to.*

Why wouldn't you tell me? I don't understand.

Aunt Elizabeth only saw the identity of the young girl. You.

But the young man was unknown. I wanted to believe it was Jacob, but what if it was not? There is significant danger in revealing a seer's prophecy to a subject when there are unknowns. You may have inadvertently tried to influence the outcome in the way of your own heart's choosing. And if we were wrong, and it was not Jacob... the results could have been calamitous.

Why are you now so sure it's him?

Certain details came together. The castle. The green hills. I then sought final confirmation from Jasper's sister, Imogen, a seer even more powerful than my sister was. She confirmed it. Jacob is your lord, Amelia. He is yours, and you are his, and together, you will do great things. Things of significant importance. But the road ahead will not be tranquil. More than this, Imogen couldn't say, because the outcomes were unclear. Rest easy now, daughter, knowing your love for Jacob is not simply powerful, but is in fact, your destiny.

Amelia drew a deep breath. "When I was a girl, I spent most of my time drawing. The same things all girls draw, I guess. Flowers, trees, mountains. But when I was five, I gave those things up for something different."

Jacob continued caressing her hair, watching her with a hazy, whimsical smile. His kind eyes urged her on.

"There was a stone castle, reaching far into the sky. Inside, was a girl with long silver hair and sad blue eyes, sitting in the window like Rapunzel. When my mother asked about her, I said the girl was trapped there. Had been for many years. The drawings continued, each similar but showing the girl's life over time, as she aged. The grasses grew taller, the weeds unruly. Always green, lots of green. Finally, the drawings stopped when I drew a great lord, who came to rescue the imprisoned maiden. Together, the lord and lady did more than live happily ever after, though. They saved the kingdom, and restored peace to the warring lands. Of course, that's when the drawings stopped."

He smiled. "Sounds like the romantic imagination of many young girls."

"The drawings weren't the end. My Aunt Elizabeth observed this same sequence, in the form of her dream prophecies. She told my mother about them when I was a girl, but my mother told her to keep it to herself, to protect me. My aunt's prophecies were always true, as you know, but Mom feared what it might mean, without context."

Jacob pulled her closer. "I'll happily fulfill this prophecy, *Blanca,*" he vowed, rewarding her with a kiss for each of his words, "though Ireland no longer needs saving."

"Ireland isn't our kingdom, Jacob," she replied, looking up at him.

He beamed down at her with understanding. "Your family."

Amelia nodded. "*Our* family."

"Of course, *Blanca.*"

"And don't you see? My drawings. Your imagination. My aunt's dreams. My cousin's vision. They're all the same story. Except you're not meant to save me from some fictional castle. You've showed me how to get past my own, internal prison. You've freed me. And now, our story really begins."

He released her hair, watching her with a thoughtful gaze. There was no doubt in his eyes, only a desire to understand. "But what does it mean? What are we meant to do?"

"I don't know yet," she admitted. The strange dreams she'd been having added to the mystery, as though there ought to be a connection, if only she could see it. With a resigned sigh, she continued, "But I know the Curse was nothing compared to the darkness ahead. The conception of Ana's son was the beginning, but events are in motion now, and they can't be stopped." She pressed her face to his chest, comforted by the strong beat of his heart. "What I do know is that we're meant to be a big part of what's to come. You and I."

He nibbled her lower lip playfully. "The Donnellys are fighters."

In the distance, the bells of the cathedral rang midnight. The witching hour.

She lifted herself to her toes, returning the bite. "Indeed they are. But for now, the lady demands her lord's marriage bed."

His eyes twinkled with his smile. "Or what?"

Amelia twisted her hands through his unruly hair and winked. "Or you may find yourself ensnared in a fight you can't *possibly* win."

"My will is yours, *Blanca,*" Jacob whispered between his wife's parted lips. "Now and always. *Síoraíocht, a stór.*"

Amelia started to ask, when he began speaking Gaelic, what the words meant.

Then she realized, she already knew.

THE STARS TWINKLED; THE HILLS SIGHED. MILES AWAY, QUINLANS sang the ancient song of Cianán and Cerridwen with joy, and an eye to the beautiful and terrifying inevitabilities ahead.

A sacred vow united, then sundered, two races, and the Deschanels are caught in the middle. They'll fight the battle from the homefront, and now a new world, Farjhem, where Ana, Aidrik, and Finn's alliance with the unreliable Agripin will either be their salvation... or the final act in their destruction.

Don't miss a minute. Download ***Empire of Shadows*** today.

Been waiting to know about Ana, Finn, Aidrik, and their unborn child? Read further for an excerpt.

EMPIRE OF SHADOWS EXCERPT

FINNEGAN
SCOTTISH HIGHLANDS

The further they hurried, the more challenging it grew to bear Anasofiya's weight. An hour ago, she'd lost all ability to carry herself forward, and Finn and Aidrik now took this burden, in a mix of love and fear. Their speed had only slowed some; though they needed to be gentle with her, in her delicate state, as it would be worse if she were to give birth in the glen.

"Not much further," Finn assured, but he was frowning. How many years had it been, since he'd seen his grandfather? Ennis St. Andrews was a man who lived today much the same as he'd lived during his childhood. The beastly wilds of the Highlands were more appealing to him than the bustling activity of nearby Inverness. His hundreds of acres protected him from the outside world, but that same safety net was now becoming a hindrance as the three rebels searched for shelter. *I was a child, last time I hiked this with Dad and Mom. Oh, I should have considered a map!*

But when was there time?

"How sure are you of this location?" Aidrik remarked, as Ana cried softly against his shoulder. Her belly was now so distended Finn feared it might erupt like an angry blister. Though Aidrik's intervention had awakened most of the Empyrean within her, there was enough human left to deeply concern both men. The few stories which existed of human women bearing Empyrean children had not ended well, for mother or child.

"Sure enough to risk the life of my wife and son. Is that what you're asking?" Finn barked. He had enough pressure on his shoulders with this endeavor, and did not need this archaic creature reminding him of the risks.

"Emotion will not serve us well, at this hour," Aidrik calmly reminded him.

Finn thought it better not to respond, instead willfully shutting out the heartrending echoes of Ana's cries to focus on the other, helpful sounds around him. Of the whispers in the trees, and the low hum of creatures inhabiting this stretch of land. Sounds which might save her.

Help me find my seanair, he pleaded. These abilities, the keener version of the connection with nature he'd always had, were still taking form. Finn understood, though, that he could speak with the trees. Could converse with the wildlife. Whatever gift Aidrik had given him, it included the ability to beseech all the colors and senses to help him find his grandfather.

The wind whipped through tall trees, creating a shimmering blanket of songs above them. The stretch of forest through which they walked remained still, other than the sounds Finn now fixated on.

A tiny fox emerged from behind a tree, halting before the small party. His tiny, black eyes blinked repeatedly as he observed them in silence. Then, the fox leapt away in a low sprint, looking back to see if the men were following. Finn's heart surged, as he realized what was happening.

"Go, this way!" Finn cried as a new energy coursed through him.

Aidrik raised an eyebrow, but said nothing. Their pace quickened as the fox wove them down a path Finn did not remember; hopefully, a quicker route, as he knew Ana did not have much time left. Aleksandr could make his entrance at any moment. And while Finn's nearly ninety-year-old grandfather could do little to help, Finn knew access to a warm hearth, and clean water, was what they needed to save the lives of both Ana and her unborn son. Healing could only reach so far.

A hospital had always been out of the question. Aleksandr would grow to the size of a child within days, and, in a matter of weeks, would resemble a young man. Their path had forever been limited by this secret, and they were banking their solace on the vague memories Finn had of Ennis St. Andrews regaling his grandson with stories of Highland fairies, magic, and lore. Finn hoped if his grandfather could believe in those things, perhaps this would not be such a stretch.

Finally, the forest grew less dense, and the ground beneath them transitioned from condensed foliage to a deep, emerald moss. A clearing lay ahead, and a small house sat cocooned in the middle. There was no stopping point for the moss, which traveled from the forest floor all the way up the sides of the tiny thatched cottage, broken only by strands of ivy woven up and around. *A lot smaller than I remembered... but it has been over twenty years, I suppose.*

They started their approach, just as a door creaked open. Ana sounded the last of her tortured cries, as her head fell back over Aidrik's arms, surrendering to her pain.

Before Finn could check on her, a tall shadow appeared in the doorway, revealing a young woman in a billowing dress. She looked familiar; like a memory.

"Come," she ushered, her expression kind. "We must hurry!"

Pick up your copy of *Empire of Shadows* now, and have it ready to curl up at your next reading session!

ALSO BY SARAH M. CRADIT

KINGDOM OF THE WHITE SEA

Kingdom of the White Sea Trilogy

The Kingless Crown

The Broken Realm

The Hidden Kingdom

The Book of All Things

The Raven and the Rush

The Sylvan and the Sand

The Altruist and the Assassin

The Melody and the Master

The Claw and the Crowned

THE SAGA OF CRIMSON & CLOVER

The House of Crimson and Clover Series

The Storm and the Darkness

Shattered

The Illusions of Eventide

Bound

Midnight Dynasty

Asunder

Empire of Shadows

Myths of Midwinter

The Hinterland Veil

The Secrets Amongst the Cypress

Within the Garden of Twilight

House of Dusk, House of Dawn

Midnight Dynasty Series

A Tempest of Discovery

A Storm of Revelations

A Torrent of Deceit

The Seven Series

1970

1972

1973

1974

1975

1976

1980

Vampires of the Merovingi Series

The Island

and more

The Dusk Trilogy

St. Charles at Dusk: The Story of Oz and Adrienne

Flourish: The Story of Anne Fontaine

Banshee: The Story of Giselle Deschanel

Crimson & Clover Stories

Surrender: The Story of Oz and Ana

Shame: The Story of Jonathan St. Andrews

Fire & Ice: The Story of Remy & Fleur

Dark Blessing: The Landry Triplets

Pandora's Box: The Story of Jasper & Pandora

The Menagerie: Oriana's Den of Iniquities

A Band of Heather: The Story of Colleen and Noah

The Ephemeral: The Story of Autumn & Gabriel

Bayou's Edge: The Landry Triplets

For more information, and exciting bonus material, visit www.sarahmcradit.com

ABOUT THE AUTHOR

Sarah is the USA Today and International Bestselling Author of over forty contemporary and epic fantasy stories, and the creator of the Kingdom of the White Sea and Saga of Crimson & Clover universes.

Born a geek, Sarah spends her time crafting rich and multilayered worlds, obsessing over history, playing her retribution paladin (and sometimes destruction warlock), and settling provocative Tolkien debates, such as why the Great Eagles are not Gandalf's personal taxi service. Passionate about travel, she's been to over twenty countries collecting sparks of inspiration, and is always planning her next adventure.

Sarah and her husband live in a beautiful corner of SE Pennsylvania with their three tiny benevolent pug dictators.

www.sarahmcradit.com

www.ingramcontent.com/pod-product-compliance
Lightning Source LLC
Chambersburg PA
CBHW020334310726
48979CB00015B/2364/J
* 9 7 8 1 9 5 8 7 4 4 0 5 5 *